HEARTS

We Claim

CHRISTINA BERRY

Published by PVR Publishing

Edited by Christina Consolino

Cover illustration by Novinkina Xeniya

Cover formatting by Sarah Kil Creative Studio

NOTE FROM THE AUTHOR

In general, *Hearts We Claim* is a lighthearted love story with several sexy bits. However, some scenes might be upsetting. This book contains homophobia, gore related to a dog bite, a family member death from cancer, child abuse (mentioned), conversion therapy (mentioned), animal neglect and cruelty (mentioned).

Also, there's cussing and fucking.

Enjoy!
Christina

CHAPTER 1
ADAM

The sun beats down on the shoulders of my dress blues, baking me like a potato wrapped in foil. God, it's hot out here. And that's saying a lot, considering it's my day job to walk through fire.

But it's not the weather that's the problem, it's the formality. These pristine white gloves, the neat rows of brass buttons down the front of my jacket, the crisply ironed pleats of my pants, and the regal Pershing cap on my head have me sweating.

I'm a casual guy. Most of the time, my job lets me relax in cargo pants and a FIRE T-shirt. But today, I've had to haul my dress blues out of deep storage to stand here, looking stoic and professional for the ceremony.

Rows of plastic folding chairs dot the neat lawn in front of the gazebo bandstand, which sits in the center of the park between Krause's historic library and city hall. Friends, family, and neighbors fill the seats. Peeking out from beneath the shadowy brims of cowboy hats, moving the air with hand fans, they watch our pomp and circumstance with community pride. And there is a good reason to be proud. Today is a big day for the Krause Fire Department.

My compatriots and I stand in two perfectly neat lines beside the bandstand, while up on the platform, Fire Chief "Big Mac" McKenna announces his successor: Watts. Well, he's Chief Watson now, but he'll always be Watts to us. When Big Mac caved to the pressure from his wife to finally retire, there was no doubt who he and the city would name as the next chief.

Watts has worked in fire service for twenty years, he's earned this promotion, and he's the first person of color to hold the top job. It's big news in this small town. Dee's fiancé, Rico, is here to report the story for the local paper, and I stand extra tall for the photos. Watts is making history today, and it couldn't be more well deserved.

With a plaque, a solid handshake, and a hearty back pat, the job passes from Big Mac to Watts, and the community erupts in applause. Drew, Dee, and I join the rest of the fire department with loud whoops and hollers in celebration.

Once the event is behind us, and we've posed for photos and mingled with the attendees for a while, I pocket my gloves and tuck my Pershing cap under my arm as I find my fire crew and their families in the shade of a nearby oak tree. Watts's wife beams at her husband as she asks if we're coming over to their house for the pool party.

We all answer in some form of the affirmative as we watch Mateo and Aaliyah, Rico's son and Watts's daughter, play chase on the wide green lawn. When we split up and walk toward our vehicles, I'm already stripping out of my clothes. I've slipped off my jacket and tugged my tie loose before I've even made it to my truck. Once I get there and pop the door open, I strip out of the rest. Toeing my patent leather shoes off and slipping out of my socks, too, I stand barefoot in the street and pull off my pants. I'd worn a pair of swim trunks rather than boxer briefs under my uniform for precisely this reason: rapid costume change.

I slide my feet into an old pair of sneakers, toss my fancy dress clothes onto the passenger seat, and pull myself up on the running board to get into the driver's seat. But when I reach for the door to pull it shut, I pause.

I'm being watched. Frowning just a little, I turn to stare at a guy who stands at the corner of Main and Vine. At his feet sits a well-behaved, large-breed dog—a pit bull lab mix, if I had to guess.

I grin at the dog, then look up and hold the man's gaze, grinning a little at him too. He's just watched me strip mostly naked. And, even after I've caught him staring, he doesn't look away. His brilliant blue eyes—which I can see in surprising detail, even from across the street—practically gleam with humor and…is that curiosity? A small smirk stretches across the man's handsome face, and I'm mesmerized.

Who is this guy? Krause is a small town, and you can be damn sure I know everyone here, especially a seriously fine man like this. I'm certain I've never laid eyes on him. I'd have remembered that mouth and the dark tousled hair. And those eyes—Jesus those eyes are like sapphires sparkling in the sunlight.

He keeps staring. And I keep staring back at him. Clearly, he's curious, and so am I. But the connection between us is severed when he looks down at his phone and turns to answer it. Disappointment sinks into my chest, but I don't let it linger.

Today is a beautiful day, and I'm late for a party. With a shrug, I shut the door, crank the engine, and head west to Watts's place.

I drive with the windows down, enjoying the refreshing breeze. It's a hot day for mid-October, but that's never bothered me. I'm a Texas boy through and through; I can handle a little heat.

Watts lives in the newer part of town, where, fifteen years back a small development of acreages replaced an old ranch. Folks around here still call this area the "old Koenig farm" instead of its fifteen-year-old name, "Pleasant Valley Estates." But things move slowly here, and everything that's happened since the turn of the twenty-first century, was "just yesterday."

Cars dot the driveway and the road around me, and I recognize most of them. All my crew mates and their partners are here, as well as a lot of folks from other shifts at Station 31 and other stations around the county.

I walk around to the back of the house, letting myself through the gate and heading toward the chatter of revelers and the squeal of children. Watts's backyard is lovely, the reason they bought the house. Wide and private, it's ringed by spindly oaks and mesquite trees, and at its center, the crystalline water of a swimming pool glimmers in the sun.

As an adult, I know I should head over to where the grownups have gathered around the grill and cocktail table to chitchat. But my inner child can't pull his attention from the sparkling water or pass up the opportunity to make an unforgettable entrance to the party.

From a good fifty feet away, I take off at a sprint across the lawn. At the last moment, I leap into the air, pull one knee to my chest, and, with a Braveheart battle cry, execute a perfect cannonball, coming down with a massive splash.

When I pop back up, I'm greeted by the sounds of applause and excited squeals from the kids dog-paddling around me in the pool. I give everyone a big dumb grin and announce, "Let the party begin!"

Several adults point out that the party already started without me, but the kids are delighted by my entrance. Mateo and Aaliyah and their friends swim around me, asking how they can do cannonballs as big as mine. I use the opportunity to impart some wisdom. "You've gotta grow big and strong like me," I flex a bicep to demonstrate, "so eat all your vegetables. Got it?"

The kids crinkle their noses at the thought of vegetables and chatter among themselves, comparing the strength of their little arms. I swim to the ladder to hoist myself out, only just now realizing I forgot to take off my shoes before diving in. Thank the baby Jesus I left my phone and wallet in the truck.

As for my sneakers, they've been through worse. I kick them off and leave them in the sun to dry. Shaking the water out of my curly hair like a shaggy dog, I wiggle my fingers in my ears to unclog them. Drew has pulled a beer from the cooler and offers it my way, so I walk to him and gladly accept. We clink bottles as I take my place among the adults.

"Girl, you should see him. I was like, 'you can check my pussy anytime,' " Chloe says to Dee with a laugh shared between them, and Drew, Rico, and I all turn to stare, wide-eyed.

"What?" Drew asks for everyone, but mostly for himself and his sole claim on Chloe's pussy.

"The new vet. I took Bodhi and Utah for their shots on Thursday, remember?"

"Yeah, and what does that have to do with checking *your* pussy?"

Chloe laughs and throws her arms around Drew's neck, teasing as she says, "Bodhi is your pussy, and Utah is mine, and when we get married, they'll be our pussies."

Drew smiles wide. He does that every time she talks about the wedding and marriage. I never would have pegged Drew for a romantic, but he's such a smitten kitten when it comes to Chloe.

Then Chloe tacks on, "Also, the new veterinarian in town is sexy as hell. I invited him to our wedding, so you'll get to meet him soon."

Drew's smile sinks into a frown, and Chloe giggles as she kisses his sour puss away.

Rico glances over to Dee. "Have you invited him to our wedding too?"

"Not yet, but I will. Gives me another excuse to watch him play with our pussies."

Rico laughs, and the two happy couples get cuddly with their canoodling. It's been a few months since Drew and Chloe and Rico and Dee got engaged in a dual dancing proposal, which I helped choreograph, and I could not be happier for them. But, sometimes it's difficult being the odd man out. Forever the single guy, the gay guy, the sidekick, and friend.

I wander to where Watts is explaining the best way to grill burgers.

"You want your meat juicy, don't you?" Watts sounds like a drill sergeant as he breathes down the dude's neck. "So don't press them too hard."

"Nothing better than juicy meat," I quip as I approach and give the guy a proper once-over as he cooks the hamburger patties to Watts's exacting specifications. He looks to be in his early twenties, slightly taller than my six-foot-two frame, and built like he lifts a lot of weights. He's handsome without being pretty and flashes a drop-dead gorgeous dimple in his cheek when he looks up and smiles at me.

Watts sees me, too, and raises his beer to clink against mine as I join them. "Rooster, meet Knox County. He's your new crewmate."

"Knox *County*?" I ask, amused by the name.

"Rooster?" Knox counters.

Fair point. I run my fingers over my damp red hair, and he nods, understanding. People have been calling me Rooster since I was born with a head of red curls. My hair isn't carrot-colored these days, more of a deep burnt-umber shade, and I keep my tight curls cut into a wide, low-maintenance mohawk so it doesn't slow me down when donning my bunker gear. Still, it's never difficult for people to understand where the nickname comes from.

"Welcome," I say to Knox, and we clink bottles. I could ask him more about his own name, but I'll save it for our next shift. "Guess I'll be seeing you at the station tomorrow."

With another nod, we all turn our attention to the grill and talk about the weather. No shop talk for now; there will be plenty of time for that when he's learning the ropes on the job.

"Good girl! You're doing so well," I coo at Drusilla.

She glances over her shoulder to give me a goofy grin—her left ear flopping with her strides as she matches my pace—then turns her attention back to the road as she runs beside me, careful not to get ahead and pull the leash. I'm impressed.

Mom's newest rescue is a Shepherd and Rottweiler mix who was removed from a hoarder with dozens of neglected and malnourished dogs in his yard. Drusilla was just a puppy, barely weaned, when she came to Mom's shelter, and already she'd suffered far too much. She had worms, fleas, and part of her tail was missing, probably bitten off by an older dog in the horde.

In the month and a half since Mom took her in, she's grown by leaps and bounds. Her coat has come in thick and lustrous, and she has tons of energy, always wiggling and wagging that nubby little tail. She's adorable and a very sweet girl with a chill disposition that makes her my favorite jogging companion.

At Main Street, we wait for the light to turn green. I run in place, while Drusilla follows my command to sit, looking dainty and desperate for a treat. Tossing her the liver morsel she's earned, I laugh when she swallows it whole. "Try savoring those treats every once in a while, Pretty Girl."

Drusilla yawns at me in response. When the light changes, and I stride forward, her excitement gets the better of her, and she darts ahead, tugging a little. I give a little tug back, reminding her who's controlling the pace. She takes the hint and slows to be at my side.

We jog past the courthouse and library, the two oldest and prettiest buildings in town. I take a deep breath of the mild morning air. Fall comes late to Texas, so any decrease in the temperature is greatly welcome.

The refreshing weather gives me a smile, and everything seems right with the world. But, when I turn at the corner to loop around the courthouse and head back home, it all goes horribly wrong.

Drusilla spots another dog coming our way, and in that instant she forgets all her training and darts forward to greet the other animal. I'm caught off guard as she tangles us in the other dog's leash and runs me right into the other dog's dad.

We collide hard, two objects in motion that have suddenly stopped. Jolted and irritated, I cuss up a storm. Of course, I don't cuss at the dog —she's young and learning. I'm the one to blame for not paying better attention, for not holding the leash more firmly. Then I look up and cuss for an entirely different reason.

"Fuck," I mutter as I catch sight of the person I've run into. Those eyes. That smirking grin. That tousled dark hair. It's him, the guy from the award ceremony, the one who watched me strip half naked.

Damn. He's handsome. Up close now, I can really see his eyes, such a luscious blue. And his hair—dark curls that wave in the breeze. My heart stutters in my chest, and I say it again, "Fuck... I mean... Sorry."

He chuckles as we manage to disentangle, and God that feels like a loss. His body felt so warm and solid against mine, and now there's just air, crisp fall air devoid of the heat I was enjoying only moments ago.

"Looks like they've made friends," the stranger says and directs my attention to the dogs. They're sniffing each other all over and whining with excitement. An instant connection for them. Puppy love at first sight.

I look back at the man standing so close. Good God, he's beautiful, and he just keeps smiling at me. *Instant connection.*

"I'm Markus." He offers his hand to shake.

I take it. Of course I take it; I will take anything this man gives me.

"Rooster," I say back.

"Rooster?" His brow furrows, and damn, even that looks good on him.

I smirk and use my free hand to gesture at my hair, stroking my fingers over the mohawk of auburn curls. "Like the red comb on a rooster's head."

"Ah, gotcha."

Do you though? Do you got me? I'm definitely game.

For some reason, I just start talking, telling him more about myself than he needs to know. "My real name is Adam, but everyone calls me Rooster—they have since I was born. I think it's a combination of the red hair and the fact I woke my parents up screeching to the sun in the wee hours of the morning."

Markus laughs, a lot. God, that laugh. It rumbles through me like thunder and pours over me like rain.

I try to think of more funny things to say, but I'm lost for words. And all at once I realize we're still shaking hands and standing awkwardly close together. Markus notices, too, retracting his hand and taking a step back.

With a commanding voice, he says, "Rufus, heel."

My body reacts to his strong tone. My mouth waters, and shivers run down my spine as my cock nearly stands at attention. I've never had a thing for dominant men, but right now, I'm definitely feeling the exception to that rule.

Markus's dog responds well too. The gorgeous pit bull mix pulls away from Drusilla and sits beside Markus. Drusilla is far less behaved when I try the same command on her, but eventually she sits with a whine.

"Rufus, good name," I say to fill the silence.

Markus smiles in response and nods to the dog at the end of my leash. "And this is?"

"Drusilla."

He furrows his brow and asks, "As in Caligula's sister?"

"Uh…" Caligula's sister? Interesting. Hot and smart. Check and check! "No, my mom is just a big *Buffy the Vampire Slayer* fan."

"Your mom named your dog?"

Okay, this conversation has gone sideways. I try to right it with another wordy monologue. "Drusilla is not my dog. She's a rescue. My mom runs a dog shelter and boarding facility on the north side of town. When I jog, I like to take a dog or two with me, to give them a chance to stretch their legs and socialize." I glance down at Drusilla, who has shifted onto her back so she can lick her genitals while she looks over at Rufus. *Uh…* Shaking my head in amusement, I look back at Markus and change the subject. "So what about you? Are you named after Marcus Aurelius?"

Markus lets out another deep, rumbly laugh. The sound does funny things to my nervous system, and my cock.

"No." His laugh turns a little wispy, like there's no air behind it. "My parents named me Mark after the Gospel of Mark, but I like Markus better."

Interesting. Everything about this guy is interesting.

Seeming anxious to change the subject, he turns his attention to Drusilla and gives her a toothless grin as he asks, "May I pet her?"

"Absolutely. She has a wonderful temperament."

Markus crouches to scratch Drusilla behind the ears, both the one that stands tall and the one that flops over a little. She whines with puppy exuberance, her stubby tail swishing a small patch of the pavement clean as she works hard to keep her butt on the ground despite all the excitement.

"You're a good girl, aren't you, Drusilla?" Markus coos, and she's clearly smitten.

Drusilla tries to lick his mouth, but he expertly dodges her tongue as he smiles up at me. Jesus, he's sexy when he's down on his knees, doling out praise, those blue eyes staring up at me,—

Markus straightens to his full height. I'm relieved and a little disappointed at the same time. He's a hair taller than me, and our eyes lock as we both smile, silent for a moment, just staring.

This is a new experience for me—to be so attracted to someone here in Krause. I'm well known as the only gay man in this very small town, at least the only *outwardly* gay man. When I'm in the mood to hook up, I drive an hour out of town to San Antonio or Austin just to flirt like this.

I like it, this notion of a local crush, and I want to explore it. I'm about to ask if Markus wants to get a coffee sometime, maybe jog together; I could give him a tour of the town. But he interrupts my thoughts when he clears his throat and says, "Well, I best be off. I need to open the clinic at nine."

"Clinic?"

Markus nods and pats his pooch on the head. "Main Street Vet Clinic. We just opened last week."

Of course! Markus is the new veterinarian who has all the local pussies purring. That conversation at Watts's promotion party makes much more sense now.

"Good to know," I tell him. "When Doc Evans retired and shut down the vet clinic, my mom had to take her dogs to Dripping Springs for shots and neutering. She fosters dogs, so it will be wonderful to have a local vet again."

"Great," Markus says, but he doesn't move to leave.

Neither do I. "Great," I mimic, and we both nod.

"Well," Markus breaks our eye contact, looking down at Rufus and giving his head a little pet as he says, "Let's go." Then to me, he adds, "It was nice to meet you, Adam."

Adam. He called me Adam. I melt from the inside out at the sound of my name on his lips. No one ever calls me by my name. It feels strange and special. Like, with him, I'm a whole different person.

"It was nice meeting you too, Markus. I'm sure we'll cross paths again."

"Looking forward to it," he says to me, then clucks his tongue at his dog. Rufus springs to his feet, and the two of them jog away, around the corner and out of sight.

Drusilla and I watch them go, then Drusilla makes a little whining sound that I feel in the depths of my soul. "Same, girl. Same."

CHAPTER 3
MARKUS

I smile down at Rufus, who grins up at me as we jog away from Adam and Drusilla.

What was *that*?

A surprise is what it was. Adam stopped me in my tracks, literally, sure, but in other ways too. I've never felt anything close to the intense attraction I feel for Adam.

On Saturday, when I was walking through downtown and came across the city hosting some fire-department ceremony, I noticed Adam in his formal uniform standing so tall and proud and…very handsome. Then, after the applause and back pats, I caught the real show as he stripped down to nothing but a pair of swim trunks right there in the street.

He sported a six pack that was more like a twelve pack of stunning, chiseled abs. To say the sight had given me pause is an understatement. I couldn't take my eyes off him. When he caught me watching, he grinned. Sweet lord that wicked grin.

Then my phone chimed with a new voicemail from my mother, and that was the cold shower I needed to stop ogling the stranger. But now, I jogged right into him. Met him and his dog in a tangle of leashes—

Heh. Sounds like some sort of kink: tied in leashes. My mind wanders to a few new places with that image in my head. Jogging faster, I try to outrun my thoughts.

Of course, I can't. I never can.

Rufus and I finish our run at the steps of the apartment above the veterinarian clinic. *Home Sweet Home*, reads the kitschy little flag next to my door. It's so cheesy, but it makes me smile every time I see it. The *But First, Pray* sign the former residents hung in the kitchen is less endearing.

When I first explored leasing this building, I couldn't see past the shortcomings of the musty old clinic with its outdated technology. It was in desperate need of a top-to-bottom rehabilitation. I decided it was not the place for me, but then the realtor mentioned that it came with fully furnished living quarters upstairs. My small business loan was only going to stretch so far, and the prospect of paying rent on top of loan payments was daunting. The moment I walked into this place with its retro decor and sunny yellow kitchen, I knew: this would be my home. Signed the papers that very day.

I hang Rufus's leash by the door and head to the kitchen, pour some food for him, then jump in the shower. When I'm in my uniform of scrubs and Crocs—not particularly fashionable but comfortable for a long day on my feet and easy to clean after a shift—Rufus and I head downstairs. We each have our own routine. While I turn on the lights and sweep the floors, Rufus sniffs.

He walks from room to room, inspecting the large animal pens that sit empty and unused, waiting for clients who need a place to board their animals when they go on vacation. Does anyone vacation away from Krause though? So far, I haven't gotten that impression.

In the lobby, I set a pot of coffee to brew, a perk for clients and a way to liven up the aromas in this place. Less musty, wet-dog stench, more fine-roasted goodness. With the new smells, the burned-out light-bulbs replaced, and the coat of dust scrubbed off the surfaces, it looks almost nice in here, comfortable, at least.

At the front desk, I grab the phone and rest it in the crook of my shoulder to listen to the after-hours messages. There are three, mostly people asking long-winded questions about my services. Simultaneously, I fire up the old computer to check my schedule for the day.

It's going to be a busy one. There's my interview with a candidate for the receptionist position, plus four cats and eight dogs scheduled for wellness checks and vaccinations. Also, I'm meeting with the guy who said he and his brother could paint this place for me.

As I continue to listen to messages, I turn to my new filing cabinet to pull out the paper records I've made for my appointments—until I can make this office fully digital—and get tangled in the long, twisted phone cord. It's a fresh reminder that I need to talk to telecom vendors about upgrading the computing and phone systems in this place.

The last call is from Kailee, my receptionist job applicant, informing me we'll need to reschedule her appointment because "something came up." Not a good sign. When I hang up the phone, I've managed to tie myself in a knot with the cord. My mind flashes back to that glorious entanglement of leashes. A much better predicament than I find myself in now.

I can picture Adam so perfectly; his gorgeous green eyes, red-tinged hair cut into a low mohawk, and that heart-stopping smile. His smile hasn't been far from my thoughts since I first laid eyes on him. But this morning's entanglement was different, so close, almost intimate. He's so big, too, like a lumberjack with thick, axe-swinging arms. His smell though—that's what surprised me the most. He'd been sweaty from his run, and his masculine musk was like an aphrodisiac. I'd wanted to clutch his sides, feel his powerful body beneath my fingers, and bury my face in his neck to breathe him in.

The clinic door swings open with the clatter and tinkle of the little bell over the entrance and spares me from my wandering thoughts. Rufus rises from his bed beside the front desk, meandering over to greet the tall, blonde woman and small, brunette boy who've come inside.

The woman and I stare at each other for a beat as she takes in the sight of me all tangled in the phone cord. She lifts the cat carrier she's holding out of Rufus's reach when he approaches for an inspection sniff, so he focuses on the little boy, who gleefully smiles and pats my gentle giant on the head a couple of times.

I try to gather my thoughts as I extricate my legs, saying over my shoulder, "Hi, you must be PB and J. I mean…"

When I'm finally free of the phone cord, I come out from behind the front desk, hand extended. The woman's handshake is firm, her eyes direct, and before I can correct my earlier mistake, she does it for me.

"Hi! I'm Dee, this is Mateo, and these little fluff balls"—she gestures at the cat carrier, still held aloft from Rufus—"are indeed PB and J."

I chuckle, both at the woman's forthrightness and at her cats' names. "Excellent. Come on back. Rufus, you keep an eye on things up here."

The little boy grins at the dog. "Bye, Rufus!" he says and pats his head again. Rufus loves kids and gives Mateo a face lick that sets the boy giggling as Dee leads him and the cats into the first exam room.

The kittens are nervous about the clinic. Mateo tries coaxing them out of their carrier with no luck, so Dee reaches in and pulls them out, earning a few scratches for her effort.

PB and J curl into themselves on the exam table, ears flattened and meowing with worry as they look for an exit. Now, it's Mateo who manages to soothe their nerves with pets and whispers that everything will be okay. I'm gentle, too, as I look at their teeth, eyes, and ears, palpate their lymph nodes and joints, listen to their hearts, measure their temperature, and weigh them, then consult their vaccination records. Recruiting Mateo to help, I get him to spray a little spray cheese on the table for the kittens to enjoy, then microchip them and administer their core vaccinations while they're distracted. When we're all finished, I reward the kittens with affection and a couple treats for their troubles before Dee returns them to the refuge of their carrier.

I work on updating the kittens' files, directing my questions about their health and activity level to Mateo, who is clearly the "owner" of these two adorable furballs. He speaks like a proud papa when he tells me, "They can do the whole obstacle course now, even the part near the ceiling!"

Obstacle course? As if seeing the question on my face, Dee answers,

"Drew and Chloe's cat Bodhi only has three legs, so Drew built an obstacle course for him. When we moved into the house, we kept it for PB and J."

Instantly, I remember my new three-legged patient. "Oh! I've met Bodhi. He and Utah came in last week. Great little guys." And I remember their cat mom inviting me to her—

"Which reminds me," Dee pulls an envelope out of her shoulder bag and hands it to me, "I heard Chloe invited you to her wedding. So I will too."

Dee's wedding invite reads, "About Damn Time" at the top and I wonder about the story behind that. Before I can ask, Mateo says, "I get to carry the rings!"

Dee smiles at the boy and ruffles his hair. "You have the most important job of the whole wedding."

He beams with pride. It's adorable.

Dee turns back to me. "Wear whatever you want, as long as it's white."

"White?"

"Yes, I want everyone to dress in white. It's weird, I know, but I'm the Bridezilla, and what I say goes. It's not a formal affair, so wear some tighty-whities if that's your thing."

Tighty-whities? I hesitate, insisting, "You don't even know me."

Dee laughs like my reluctance is ridiculous. "You're good with animals. That's all I need to know. And I'm sure we'll see you at Chloe and Drew's big day this weekend, right?"

This town is so odd. I've now been invited to *two* weddings, a quinceañera, and a competitive bowling league. But will the good people of Krause still welcome me with open arms when they learn I'm having lusty thoughts about one of their firefighter heroes?

Out in the lobby, the bell over the door chimes. Dee and I nod, which I guess means I'll be attending her wedding. Explaining that I'll bill her for this visit at her next one—once I've set up the accounting software—I give them courteous farewells as we leave the exam room.

In the front lobby, a small woman is losing a tug-of-war battle with a massive dog, so I hustle over to assist her. The dog seems desperate to follow Mateo out the front door. Rufus helps to run interference, and

I manage to get a hand on the leash so I can also help. "You must be Mrs. Newman."

"Och, call me Angie, please. And this here is Elsa."

After I've helped Angie maneuver Elsa into one of the exam rooms, I open my mouth to ask a few questions, but Angie keeps talking. "Elsa is a rescue, and I don't know her full history. I'm assuming she's never visited a vet. She was a mess when the shelter called to place her with us. You clean up good, don't you girl?" She bends down to say that last part to the dog and is rewarded with a sloppy kiss on the cheek. To me, she continues, "Today, I want to get her flea meds and dewormer, install a microchip, and get started on a course of vaccinations."

"Sounds good." We work together to keep Elsa calm as I perform my exam. Again, a dollop of spray cheese helps with distraction while I get her chipped and vaxxed without much trouble.

The woman keeps talking between answering my questions about Elsa's appetite and energy levels, a fount of information. "She seems fit as a fiddle to me. One of the healthiest rescues I've taken in. We—my family and I—run a dog shelter. We take in dogs who've been used in fighting or who've suffered neglect, clean them up, teach them some manners, and try to adopt them out."

I've heard this story before, just this morning. Scrunching my face in concentration, I scrutinize the details of this woman, her green eyes and graying red hair. "Are you related to Adam?"

The woman's face positively lights up. "Do you know my Rooster?"

I chuckle at the nickname and consider how to answer. *Do* I know Rooster?

Not waiting for my response, Angie jumps right in, gushing about Adam. "I'm his proud momma. He's great with the dogs, something of a dog whisperer, and he can easily handle these giant beasties since he's a big strapping firefighter..."

She keeps talking, but I'm only half listening. All I can focus on is the memory of Adam's face and the dimple in his left cheek when he smiled. It feels strange how Adam keeps popping up in my mind, in my space, and in all the spaces around me. Strange, yes, but in a good way. A very good way.

I want to ask his mom about him. She knows everything, and I want to know everything too. But I keep my questions to myself and school my reactions, plastering a thin smile on my face as I focus on my patient, efficiently performing the remainder of Elsa's exam, even as my mind wanders to places it shouldn't go.

"So tell me about you." Angie jolts me from my thoughts. "Are you single?"

"He's single, he's gorgeous, and I'm pretty sure he's gay."

"Mom."

"What?" My sweet, petite mother blinks up at me, the picture of innocence, but I know better. I can see the scheming twinkle in her eyes.

"All single attractive men are not gay."

"True. But I just think he's gay. My gaydar went off."

Oh good lord. "Mom. Gaydar is not a thing, and even if it were, I'm pretty sure you would not have it."

"I knew you were gay before your fifth birthday."

"That's different."

"Why?"

"Because I'm your son. He's a random dude."

"You wouldn't be calling him a random dude if you met him. You'd be calling him dinner."

"Mom!" I don't bother to tell her that I have met him. And yes, he is absolutely delicious to look at. She doesn't need any encouragement when she gets on one of her matchmaker kicks. Between my four sisters and me, Mom is always on the prowl for son-in-law material.

"And dessert," she adds with a wink.

"Jesus Christ. What has gotten into you?"

"I just want to see you happy."

"And you think throwing me at the town's new vet like a virginal sacrifice to a volcano will do that?"

"Well, no—we both know you're not virginal."

"What am I going to do with you?" I chuckle and roll my eyes as I wrap my arms around her and pull her against me; she's so small I can rest my chin on the top of her head.

Her arms loop around my waist, and she takes a deep breath, like she wants to inhale me. She does that a lot, with all of us kids. I think she hates the fact that we're grown adults now, even as she tries to pair us all off with mates. Mom seems to want to keep us in her nest, even as she pushes us to spread our wings and fly. It's sweet and lovable, and I squeeze her a little tighter. She spanks my ass as she pulls away with a smirk and another wink. "So, tell me about Drusilla?"

I blink at the rapid subject change as Mom leads me into the shelter kennels and over to Drusilla's enclosure. Setting my train of thought back on track, I give her a full report. "She's sweet as can be, great temperament, very adoptable." Popping the lock on her enclosure, I walk into Drusilla's pen, and she comes up on her hind legs, putting her paws on my chest and trying to lick my mouth. I dodge and weave. "Hey now, sweet girl. I don't like you like that."

Mom chuckles as she straightens up the enclosure, refilling Drusilla's water. "She's clearly crushing on you."

"She must have terrible gaydar."

In the station kitchen, I'm expecting the familiar aroma of Watts's gourmet coffee, but the percolator sits idle. Oh right. Watts is upstairs now—literally and figuratively—riding a desk in the HQ office above our firehouse. As the station closest to the county seat, we serve as the department headquarters too. But the admin and ranked officers who serve above us use their own entrance, and they have their own percolator.

It feels wrong for this place to smell like anything other than coffee, so I go on a hunt through the cabinets and drawers looking for a bag of grounds.

It's slim pickings. Watts must have taken the good stuff with him when he moved upstairs. There's an old can of coffee in the dusty forgotten back of a bottom shelf, and I grab it. When I stand, I come nearly nose to nose with a massive man.

Jesus! I stumble backward, almost dropping the coffee can and spilling its contents all over the floor.

The big guy smiles awkwardly and steps back a pace. Raising his hands he explains, "Sorry. Sorry. Didn't mean to scare you."

After a few blinks, I recognize him: Knox, the new guy. And as I make that connection, I connect his words, too, frowning as I do. Did he just suggest that he *scared* me? "You didn't—I wasn't scared, just startled…a little."

Knox's smile grows wider. He has a nice smile, one of those lazily handsome grins that usually spell trouble for me when I'm out for a night of fun. As irritated as I am, I shake it off and smile, too, as I stretch my hand out to shake. "Anyway, welcome, Probie."

His handshake is firm but not crushing, and his eye contact is steady. Not bad. I'd say we're off to a good start after that jump scare.

"Probie?"

"You're a probationary officer for the next year, so get used to the nickname and get used to saying 'Yes, sir' and 'Yes, ma'am' when we assign tasks for you to handle." I step away and stretch my arms wide. "So this is Station thirty-one. Need the tour?"

With a smile, he nods. "Sure."

"Cool. But first, make me some coffee, Probie."

His smile sinks. I raise a brow and hold the can of coffee grounds out to him, expectantly.

"Yes, sir," he says as he takes it from me and glances around for the percolator.

That's when Drew comes into the kitchen looking freshly showered —and probably freshly fucked if that smile on his face is any indication. He and Chloe are cute, still in that pre-newlywed phase of their relationship where they can't stay away from each other. He used to be the most enthusiastic fire brother in this place. Now, when it's a slow shift, I catch him checking the time on his phone, anxious to get back to his favorite person.

And wouldn't you know it, right on cue, the other newly-in-love member of our crew comes in through the bay door with a freshly fucked grin of her own. I make introductions as Dee slides her energy drink into the fridge.

"Hey, Dee, Drew, meet our new probie, Knox County. He's making coffee."

"Awesome." Dee shakes the new guy's hand before she goes into the ladies locker room to hang her bag and change from sneakers to boots.

"Are you one of the sons in County Sons Construction?" Drew asks as he extends his hand.

Knox nods. "Yes. You hired my dad and my brothers to build your house."

Drew raises a brow. "Your dad and your brothers? Hmm. So, how does your dad feel about you joining the fire service?"

Knox pulls a face and scratches the back of his neck. "He's…disappointed."

Huh. There's clearly a story there, but Knox obviously doesn't want to tell it, so I change the subject. Handing my coffee mug over, I say, "I like my coffee with one cream and one sugar."

"I…" Probie looks between me and Drew, who just stares at him expressionless, and after a moment he says, "Yes, sir."

With his lips twitching, Drew tries not to smile as he hands his mug over too. "Black for me."

Drew and I sit at the dining table as Dee comes out to join us. She's the one who asks the burning question: "Your name is Knox County? Like the actual county?"

"Yep."

I can't see Knox's face, but something in the set of his shoulders tells me he just sighed and rolled his eyes. "I mean… Yes, ma'am—"

"No! No *ma'am* with me, Probie. Just call me Dee."

Knox glances over his shoulder and nods, then gets back to work on setting the coffee to brew as he explains, "My granddad thought he was funny when he named my dad Travis County. Then Dad followed suit and did the same thing. There's Briscoe, Victoria, Clay, and me."

Wow. "Now *that* is dedication to a theme! I thought my mom Angie was weird when she gave us all A names like hers. It's Alice, Anna, Ava, and me."

"Rooster?" Drew asks with a grin.

"Adam." I smirk at him.

The coffee is quick to brew, and Knox serves us all without complaint. We let him sit for a moment, take a few sips of his own drink, then we fall into long-winded explanations about how things work around here.

Since Dee is our new LT, she does most of the talking. "Every Tuesday is Big Truck Day. Which means we wash the truck and check all apparatus. Every Wednesday is Big Clean Day, and that's when we clean the station—bathrooms, kitchen, dust, mop. Whichever team is on during those shifts handles the cleaning. Since today is Wednesday, we're doing the Big Clean. You'll clean the bathrooms."

Knox smirks but doesn't complain.

Dee asks Drew to explain the phone policy, and he's quick to do so, clearly excited that he's not the new guy anymore, and he can hand off phone patrol to the new-new guy. "When the phone rings, you answer. And if you don't pick up by the third ring, you have to give us one hundred push-ups."

I pitch in by explaining the meal calendar. Pointing to the crockpot where my world-famous—well, county-famous—jambalaya simmers, I let him know that tonight is my night for dinner. Dee and Drew both whoop with glee.

It's a slow shift, so we're able to clean the whole station and enjoy our dinner without interruption as we explain our roles. With Watts's move upstairs, we all shift seats in the truck. Dee has been promoted from chauffeur to lieutenant and takes the lead on scene now. I've moved into the driver's seat. Drew takes my old spot behind the LT, where he'll handle hydrants and hoses. And Probie gets Drew's old job on nozzle and fire suppression.

To his credit, Knox tries not to look too overwhelmed as he takes this information in with eager nods, like he'll remember it all. He won't. No one ever does. That's sort of the point. We throw everything at you, early and often, to see if you've got what it takes to stick around.

We're mostly finished with our dinner—just sitting around the table razzing Probie about all the grunt work we'll delight in assigning him—when a medical call comes in over the loudspeaker.

We come to attention—all joking aside—and give Knox clear instructions as we climb into the truck, me behind the wheel. Once everyone is strapped in and Dee has mapped the route to the address, I put the truck in gear and hit the gas. Dee slaps on the siren, and we head to our first call with our new crew in place.

CHAPTER 5
MARKUS

This is day two since I've seen him.

Not that I'm counting.

Who am I kidding? I'm absolutely counting. It's been two long days.

Too long days.

I try not to fixate on how much I want to see Adam again. It seems pathetic to jog the same path with excitement bubbling in my chest, hoping for another run-in. Still, when Rufus and I turn the corner between the library and courthouse, I find myself desperately seeking him. Rufus, too, seems anxious to scent Drusilla in the air.

But there's nothing, no one. Just empty sidewalk on this chilly fall morning.

Rufus and I pick up the pace. Last night, the weather changed when the first cold front of the season blew through town, and I switched from jogging shorts to my trusty gray sweatpants. You know, just in case. But, it's not *that* cold yet, and I'm starting to sweat.

We should get back to the clinic. This is going to be a busy day, with the painters coming this morning, twelve patient appointments, and still no receptionist. I should place an ad in the newspaper, put a sign in the window, and—

Shit!

Just as we've rounded another corner at the back of the courthouse, Rufus picks up his pace from a jog to a sprint. Before I realize what's happening, I nearly faceplant as he drags me over to a very excited and very familiar dog.

My heart stutters in my chest as I stumble and barely stop myself before running right into the man I've been desperately seeking all morning. Adam awkwardly teeters as he comes to a stop—apparently Drusilla dragged him too—and smiles so wide I wonder if he's been looking for me like I've been looking for him.

Rufus lets out a joyous bark at Drusilla, who's doing a cute little ants-in-her-pants dance, and the whole scene has me grinning like a fool. I glance up at Adam as he turns his attention toward me, taking a none-too-subtle look, lingering on my sweats. I just about swallow my tongue when I notice he's in gray sweatpants, too, and I can sort of make out the outline of his—

"Hi," he says, and I jerk my gaze up to a teasing smile pulling at his lips.

"Hey." I try to play it cool but get stuck when I can't think of anything else to say.

"What's your route?" he asks, but before I can answer, he lifts the bottom of his T-shirt to wipe some sweat off his brow, and I completely lose my mind.

He's built. Like…*really* built. I saw him strip down to his swim trunks the first time I laid eyes on him, and it sucked me in…er…I mean…captured my undivided attention. But that was from fifty feet away. Here, just a couple feet from me, within reach, his muscles look svelte, lean, and they shine with sweat—

Shit. What was his question?

Oh right, my route. "I, um, usually jog down to the river and then up and around the high school and back."

He nods his approval, then stuns me when he asks, "Mind if we join you?"

I blink down at Rufus, who is licking Drusilla's face. My sweet boy is obviously in love. With a smile, I nod. "Sure."

We turn together and head toward the river, where the trees change from red oaks and pecans to cottonwood and cypress. Down in the river bottom of the park, everything is shady and cold. The brisk air cools my sheen of perspiration and chills my breath, pricking my lungs with each sharp inhale.

It's difficult to keep up with Adam. His pace is slightly faster than I'm used to, and he hardly seems winded at all. I guess as a firefighter, he's in far better shape than, well, everyone else. But those guys have to race through fire while carrying people on their shoulders, so I can imagine this little jog of ours is child's play to him.

Curious about his career, I find my voice between huffs of air. "How long have you been a firefighter?"

He glances over like he's surprised to find me here, surprised to hear my voice after so long jogging in companionable silence. Shit. Have I ruined this thing we're sharing?

I guess not, because he answers, "About ten years. I was a fire explorer as a kid but formally joined the academy after high school graduation."

"A fire explorer?"

He nods. "It's like a club where you learn about firefighting techniques and compete in the Fire Games each year. They have an obstacle course, bunker gear drills, tower climb... It's pretty cool, and now I'm a sponsor of the local team."

"So you've always wanted to be a firefighter?"

He considers for a moment, then nods again. "I guess I have. As a kid, you see the big red truck filled with heroes who are coming to save the day, and, maybe it's an ego trip, but I wanted to be one of those guys."

"A hero," I say, and my voice sounds a little too wistful, like my breathlessness is caused by the handsome man beside me and not the fast pace of our run. It's embarrassing.

Fortunately, Adam moves the conversation along with a question of his own. "What got you into animal medicine?"

"A hero complex," I answer with a shrug.

Adam laughs, and *God* the sound of it.

I laugh a little too. "When I was eight, I rescued a bird with an injured wing and nursed him back to health. When he could fly again, he did, but he never went far, always coming back with little gifts. I felt a stronger connection with that bird than I felt with most people. So I started adopting pretty much every animal I met. When it came time to go to school, it seemed obvious what my calling was."

"Nice. That's really great."

The admiration I see in his eyes when he says that means a lot. I barely know this man, but everything I've seen from him so far suggests he's a stand-up person, and it means something to have his praise.

As we come out of the river bottom on the far side of the high school, he picks up the pace a bit, and I push myself to keep up. The dogs trot side by side ahead of us, seeming to be in heaven as they get exercise and socialization all at the same time. For Rufus, who had to leave his dog-park friends behind when we left College Station, the situation is a godsend. It's pretty nice for me too.

Adam and I don't talk much as we pass back through town toward my clinic. He's finally starting to get winded, while I'm about to pass out from running this hard. Still, I'm proud of myself for maintaining the pace and my dignity.

"Have you been in there yet?" Adam asks and points to a cute little diner in one of the old buildings on the town square. The façade is brick with tall windows across the front. Just below the roof line, a stone block reads G.W. Eaton 1902. On the side of the building, the faded design of an old ghost sign reads Eaton Hardware, hinting at the building's long retail history.

But now, a neon sign in the window indicates it's Lavern's Diner. Inside, the lights are warm, and clusters of people fill some of the booths, chatting over steaming cups of coffee and plates of warm food. My mouth waters.

"Not yet," I answer.

"Don't miss it. Lavern serves up the best breakfasts, and her chicken fried steak is second to none. Plus, they're dog friendly."

Never, not once, have I craved chicken fried steak. But the way

Adam bites his lip and moans deep in his throat has me desperate for a taste. I clear my own throat and aim for a neutral tone as I say, "Good to know."

Adam points out a few other spots: the barbershop he likes, an auto-repair place he recommends. His helpful tips blend together with the rest of my new-guy-in-town brain stew. The chances of me remembering all these details are slim.

When we reach the vet clinic, Drusilla and Adam stop to say goodbye to Rufus and me. Not sure what is appropriate in this moment, I reach out my hand to shake. Adam looks at it for a beat, then accepts my grip in his. It's awkward. So, so awkward.

I try to think of something more to say, but Adam speaks first. "Maybe we'll run into you two again tomorrow."

With a grin and a nod, I answer a little too excitedly. "Definitely. We could meet here at eight."

"Great."

"Cool." Well, shit, this is getting awkward again. *Walk upstairs. Walk upstairs. Turn around and walk upstairs!* My brain is insistent, but my feet are not cooperating, and my mouth has other ideas. "Maybe we can stop in at Lavern's for some breakfast."

Shit. Fuck. Did I just ask him out? This was just a jog. Two new friends jogging. And now, I'm trying to turn it into a meal? *Dumb!*

"Sounds great!" Adam stuns me when he smiles at the idea. "I'll meet you here at eight." With that, he starts to jog away. Drusilla is reluctant to leave, making herself into a cute little lump on the cool pavement beside Rufus, her tongue lolling out of her panting mouth. Adam turns, jogging backward in one spot as he smiles, whistles, and calls to Drusilla. "Come on girl! We'll get to see them again tomorrow."

Drusilla whines one last time, then gives in to Adam's tugs. Rufus and I watch as they jog around the corner and out of sight. Only then do I gasp for air, pretty sure I'm going to vomit from all the exercise, or maybe from all the excitement.

Holy crap. We have a breakfast date tomorrow.

CHAPTER 6
ADAM

We're early. I try not to look too anxious as I stretch at the bottom of Markus's stairs, but I've been here for several minutes. My hamstrings are loose enough.

Should I go up and ring the bell? Are they waiting inside for us? We didn't discuss that when we made this date for a run and breakfast. Though, calling it a "date" is being generous. It's a jog. Nothing more.

Never mind the way Markus's eyes shine when he smiles at me, or the way his gaze strays over my body when he thinks I'm not looking. News Flash: when it comes to him, I'm *always* looking.

But Markus is new to town. He's meeting a lot of new people. I'm just one, part of the crowd. I shouldn't read too much into anything he says or does until he's a bit more settled in Krause.

My body snaps to attention when a creak from above sounds, the old wooden door at the top of the stairs swinging open. And there stands Markus, smiling down at me. The happy gleam in his eyes looks a lot like the gleam in Rufus's eyes when he spots Drusilla. The dogs bark excitedly, their tails wagging so hard their whole bodies wiggle. Markus and I just smile a little wider at each other.

This time, when we jog, I slow my pace. It was late into our run yesterday when I realized I'd been going too fast, and Markus was struggling to keep up. Won't make that mistake again. I wouldn't want to make our runs unpleasant for him.

Switching the route a bit, too, I turn the exercise into a newcomer's tour of the town. Instead of heading toward the river and the high school like before, we make our way uphill and toward the highway. I point at the sign for Angie's Angels, with the cute little painting of a dog and a cat watching a sunset together, arm in arm. "That's my mom's place, where she runs her animal rescue, foster, and adoption programs. Mostly, she works with dogs and cats, but she's fostered a few rabbits, too, and a chicken once." The animal wasn't a chicken so much as it was a rooster with no sense of time and a bad attitude. My sisters named him Adam because they thought they were hilarious. I hated that damn bird. It's a story I'd rather not get into with Markus. Moving on… "Figured, you know, since you're the town vet, that'd be good info to have."

"Definitely." Markus nods, and sounds a lot less winded than he did yesterday. "How many animals can she house safely? And what's her intake process?" At my confused frown, he clarifies, "I just mean, where do the animals come from?"

"Ah, well, she has room for twenty-five animals, but she's taken in up to forty in emergency situations. Most of the animals are brought in by the sheriff. If they're called out for cruelty or if something's happened to an owner."

"Damn, forty animals. That's a big operation for one woman to manage alone."

I laugh at the thought of my mom ever doing anything *alone*. "She ropes us kids in for a lot of it, and there's a network of foster volunteers she works with."

"That's great. Really, truly wonderful."

Clearly, Markus and Mom could talk for hours about this, but I'm not ready to bring a boy home with me just yet, so we keep jogging until we're cutting through the packed parking lot of the Pump & Sip.

With my tour guide cap back on, I tell him: "This is a gas station that sells everything from bait and tackle to guns and ammo, plus they make exceptionally delicious kolaches. You haven't officially *lived* in Krause until you've experienced one of their jalapeño and sausage klobasneks."

"Noted," Markus says with a smile so wide his teeth glint in the rays of the morning sun. "But this morning we're checking out Lavern's place, right?"

"Right!" I beam back at him.

His enthusiasm about this breakfast of ours is contagious. Enough with the town tour—I'm ready to sit down for a meal with this man, so we head to Lavern's Diner a couple blocks away. Lavern's sister, Agnes, greets us at the door, though she greets the dogs more than us, showering them with affection before she leads us to a table by the window with a pair of massive menus.

Before we've had time to peruse them, she's back with a bowl of water for the dogs. Drusilla gulps the water too quickly and develops a case of hiccups, which thoroughly confuses Rufus. He tries to help alleviate the problem by licking her snoot. It's adorable, and I can't stop laughing at how cute the two of them are together.

I glance over at Markus to see if he's watching them, too, but instead I catch him staring at me. Quickly, he lifts his menu, studiously analyzing every line, like I didn't just catch his ogle. It gives me something new to grin about.

Mom's been bringing my sisters and me to this diner at least once a month since I was knee-high to a grasshopper, so I don't need to consult the menu to know what I want. But I can pretend. Using it to hide my smile, I watch Markus's bright blue eyes scan all the available items.

Agnes returns with a pair of waters for us humans, then pulls a pen out of her hair and clicks it into action on her pad of paper, posing, one hip angled as she waits for us to order.

Agnes and Lavern are interesting women. By all standard metrics, they are "old." But you'd never guess that by watching them. Both women move fast, work hard, and lift more than they probably should. I was once called out here because local rancher Clayton Wilson was choking on a chicken bone. Before we could even step through the door, we watched through the picture window as Agnes administered the Heimlich maneuver so effectively, it not only dislodged the food from his airway, it pulled him right off his feet, all two hundred and fifty pounds of him. Considering the woman looks like she's hardly half that, it was a sight to behold.

Now, she just looks impatient, so I quickly order my usual: scrambled eggs, sausage, half stack of pancakes, cottage cheese, and fruit. Markus grins wide as he listens to me order, then he asks for a Denver omelet and a slice of cherry pie.

Once Agnes has left, Markus and I glance down at the dogs, who are lying so close that their noses and paws touch. Markus chuckles at the sight, and the sound is so comforting, like hot chocolate...sipped in front of a fireplace...while cuddled under a blanket on a cold winter night. I shiver at the warm thoughts and try to tamp down the desperate sense of need the imagery evokes inside me.

Fortunately, Markus distracts me from that train of thought, still talking about the dogs. "How old is Drusilla?"

I shrug. "Roughly six months. Mom took her in when she was rescued from an overcrowded puppy mill just south of here about six weeks ago, but you'd never guess from her temperament. Very chill dog, at ease around other animals and children too. I'm shocked she hasn't been adopted yet."

"She's not your dog?"

"Oh. No. I don't have any pets. But I help Mom out with the dogs from the shelter when I can."

"I've been meaning to mention... I met your mom when she brought in Elsa a couple days ago."

I smile, remembering my conversation with Mom about her gaydar. "Yes, she was very impressed by you."

"Well...that's...good to hear." Why is he being bashful? And why is his bashfulness so cute? "Your mom seems like a very nice person."

Of course she was nice to him. She sees son-in-law potential in Markus. She did this with my sister Alice's husband. Theirs was a mom-falls-first romance if I ever saw one. "Angie Newman is a force of nature, but she's a force for good."

Markus laughs, and he looks like he has follow-up questions, but Agnes picks that moment to come out of the kitchen, her arms laden with plates, aiming for our table. We wait as she sets everything down. When she asks, we assure her we're good. She sets down a plate of chicken chunks, rice, and a little pumpkin puree for the dogs then leaves us all to our meals.

Markus's omelet is about as big as my forearm and packed full of diced peppers, cheese, and ham, and his slice of pie is a quarter of a pie tin. My plate, too, is heaped with a little extra of everything I ordered. Agnes is always keen to keep us firefighters well-fed. "You need the calories," she insists when we tell her it's too much.

I watch Markus take his first bite. Surprisingly, it's not the omelet but the pie he goes for first, and I delight in the look of pleasure on his face. The accompanying sound he makes in the back of his throat sends a shiver through me.

Turning my attention to my own food, I can't help myself when I make similar sounds of pleasure, finding the food especially delicious today. Reaching for my water, I glance up and notice that Markus is watching me too now.

I grin and purse my lips around my straw, sucking the icy water deep and swallowing hard. Markus's cheeks redden, and he glances away, back to his food, stuffing a big bite in his mouth. Very interesting. I'm not sure which is more fascinating: his shyness or my body's feral reaction to his shyness.

After a moment more of the weighty silence between us, I ask, "What brought you to Krause?"

I've been wondering for a while. This isn't the sort of town that people move to. Mom calls it a "Mellencamp town." Most of us were born in this small town, we've lived here all our lives, and we'll probably die here too. Apparently, Krause has a newcomers club. Chloe joined it when she moved back and told me that some of the "newcomers" had lived here for over thirty years.

Markus swallows the food he's been chewing. "I went to vet school at A&M and completed a residency in College Station, but after that I was keen to open a practice of my own. Saw an ad for the clinic for rent here in Krause, and after doing some research realized there's no other clinic within a twenty-mile radius, so I was keen to serve this community. Plus, the rent is cheap, and the clinic came with a free apartment, so…" He shrugs and stuffs another bite of pie in his mouth.

I laugh, loving the cheeky grin he gives me. "Have you had a lot of business?"

Markus nods. "Gobs. Krause loves its animals."

"That it does." I scratch behind Drusilla's floppy ears. "Where's your family?"

Markus blanches, his face draining of color, and I wonder if something terrible has happened to them. Cancer? A housefire? Swarm of killer bees? But when he opens his mouth to answer, there's none of the doom and gloom I was anticipating. "They're in Mineral Wells."

"Is that the town with that massive old hotel at the center?"

He chuckles. "Yep. The Baker Hotel."

I notice he doesn't leave much room for a conversation about his family in that response. So I ask more about him. "Did you grow up there?"

"Yeah." That one little word seems to convey so much with the dark bitterness of its tone, and it's something I'd like to explore. But he quickly changes the subject back to me. "Have you always lived in Krause?"

"Yep, my mom's family has been in Krause for three generations."

"And your dad?"

My throat closes, and the bite I was about to swallow gets stuck. Markus looks worried as I cough and sip water until I can breathe again. My reaction to his innocuous question is embarrassing, but I've lived in this town my whole life, and everyone here knows the story of my dad. I'm not accustomed to the topic coming up over breakfast.

Finally, when I can speak, I say, "He's gone."

As far as answers go, it's as vague as can be, and, Jesus, I make it sound like he's dead.

"He left," I clarify, though, it's not much clarity at all. But I'm not ready to tell the whole story just yet. And it's clear Markus isn't ready to share his family stories yet either, so we turn our attention to the dogs. I remark, "I think they're dating."

Markus laughs again, and any residual dark emotions are burned away with the lightness of the day and the dogs curled up together at our feet.

Swallowing his final bite of pie, Markus pushes the dessert plate aside and brings his other plate closer to dig into his omelet. With his first bite, he makes those sexy groans of appreciation again, and the sound sets my imagination loose. I can picture it so clearly, down on my knees before him, my palms squeezing the globes of his ass while his fingers twist in the curls of my hair. Me, sucking him deep, while he groans and moans as he comes against the back of my throat.

My imagination has me so sex drunk I almost miss it when Markus finishes his food. Pushing this plate aside, too, he reaches for the check Agnes placed upside down on the table between us. I manage to scoop it up first.

"Let me split it with you," Markus insists.

"Nonsense. This is your welcome-to-town breakfast."

I dig into my pocket for my wallet and take the opportunity to adjust the erection my thoughts have brought to life. When I'm suitable for standing, I head to the counter with Markus and the dogs following.

Lavern rings us up, asking how we liked everything. We rave about the food, and the dogs give her their thanks with a couple gentle licks and big grins.

When we've paid, I walk out to the sidewalk, stuffing my wallet back into my sweats. Markus follows, and we stretch for a few moments before we walk back toward his clinic.

"You really didn't need to buy my breakfast," he insists again.

I've always found it charming when men try to wrestle me for the check after drinks or a night out, but with Markus, I find it downright delightful. Like, maybe he'll literally wrestle me for the right to pay our way.

"You can pay next time." The moment I say the words—*next time*—I wonder if it's a mistake. Am I moving too fast, just assuming we'll eat together again? Pretty bold assumption.

Markus either doesn't sense the awkward shift in conversation, or he doesn't care. He shrugs and says, "Sure thing."

Too soon we've arrived at his clinic and the steps that lead up to his apartment. This time, he's the one who suggests we meet again. "Same time tomorrow?"

I wince. God, I wish I could. "Can't. I'm on shift this time tomorrow. We work a twenty-four/forty-eight schedule. My shift starts in a few hours, noon to noon. But I can meet you here on Thursday morning."

"Great. It's a date," he says cheerily.

I blink at him. A *date*?

Quickly, he starts to backpedal. "I just mean... We'll meet again on that date. On Thursday."

Markus's awkwardness and vulnerability are incredibly charming. But he seems uncomfortable, glancing down at his dog like he's desperate to be rescued from his rambling mouth.

Well, hey, I'm a rescuer. It's what I do. So I come to the rescue when I say with a smile, "Sounds perfect. I'll see you then..." For our *date*.

It's a *date.*

Ugh.

Those words have haunted me for nearly forty-eight hours. So dumb and silly and wrong. We're just friends jogging together. And are we even *friends* yet? We hardly know each other. We're just two dog dads taking the same route to run around town.

It's not a damn date.

And the look Adam gave me when I said it, like he was laughing at my stupid faux pas…

Ugh!

I'm still embarrassed. *Mortified.*

The thing that frustrates me most is how flustered I feel about it. This awkward guy Adam keeps encountering is *not* me. I'm not someone who fawns all over an attractive man like a lovestruck teenager. I'm patient, quiet, and calm, methodical and thoughtful in everything I do.

But tell that to my stomach right now as I shower *before* my jog with Adam and Drusilla. My insides are tied in knots, my head is a mess, and I'm hyperaware of every sound. As if I think Adam might show up early, walk right through my door, and come find me in the shower, naked and wet and thinking of him.

Rufus seems just as edgy, pacing in front of the door, anxious for our date too. When neither of us can stand it anymore, I get him into his harness and leash, and we head outside, down the stairs. I take my time stretching on the sidewalk in front of the clinic.

It's cloudy today, and the air has that portent of rain to it. I breathe in deeply, loving the charged, wet aroma of an approaching fall storm. Too warm and humid for sweatpants today, I'm in my running shorts and a blue T-shirt. I certainly did not choose blue because it looks good with my eyes. Heh. *Of course that's why I chose it. I'm so transparent—*

"Hey." Adam's voice startles me, and I spin around to see him looking good in his running shorts and tight T-shirt. It's green, like his eyes, and I grin. Maybe I'm not the only one who's being transparent here. Rufus whines and hops a little, trained not to pull on his leash but impatient to be by Drusilla's side nonetheless.

Drusilla isn't quite so well behaved, yanking on her leash as she barks dramatically. When she ignores Adam's attempts to get her to sit and stay, he gives up and lets her drag him to Rufus and me.

"Hey," I say back when he's in front of me, looking a little shiny from the run he took to meet me here.

Adam smiles, and God, he's got a great smile, a great mouth, really. I frown at that wayward, lascivious thought.

His smile sinks into a frown, too, as he looks down at Drusilla. "Well, it's official." He pets the dog while she ignores him, sniffing excitedly at Rufus. "I'm failing at these obedience lessons."

I chuckle when Drusilla mounts Rufus, and Adam tries to command her to sit. She doesn't. Rufus, on the other hand, sits perfectly still as his favorite puppy showers him with all her love and affection.

"Girl, you're lucky you're cute," Adam says with a huff. "She was doing so well, following every command, until she saw her boyfriend. Then all reason fell away, and she ran to him with needy desperation."

Girl, I can relate. I give Drusilla a couple head pats in sympathy and understanding.

Adam nods his chin toward the sidewalk, and we begin our jog, falling into an easy stride as we make our way up Main Street, past the old library, and down to the creek.

As we move, the heavy gray sky seems to bubble and froth, tendrils of wind twisting through the leaves of the sycamore trees, reaching out with chilly fingers from the advancing cold front.

This is probably not a good day for a jog. The morning weatherman was going on about a Blue Norther bringing much cooler temperatures and thunderstorms, but I ignored him. I wouldn't have missed this rendezvous with Adam for anything, and I get the impression he feels the same way.

"Are you coming to the wedding this weekend?" Adam asks. His question catches me off guard. I haven't decided what to do about the two wedding invites stuck to my fridge with the gnome magnets that came with the apartment.

"I, uh, guess?" As far as answers go, it's not my best.

Adam easily senses my hesitation and launches into his hard sell: "You should come. It'll be a blast. Drew's my fire brother, and Chloe is amazing. She's going all out with this wedding. She designed a lovely arbor for their backyard that overlooks the hills to the west. We built it last week and draped everything in little twinkle lights." He glances at me and waggles his brows as he adds, "Very romantic."

Christ on a cracker! He's gorgeous when he does that. And the likelihood of my attendance is rising with his every word.

"Plus, I look damn fine in my dress blues."

Sold! First time I laid eyes on this man, he looked stunning in his dress uniform. I'm suddenly desperate to see him in it again...and perhaps help him strip out of it too.

Still innocently talking about the wedding, Adam adds, "They made fancy little bow ties for the ringbearers—their cats, Bodhi and Utah."

I can only imagine chaos with those two ornery cats bearing the wedding rings, and I laugh at the notion. "Sounds like a good time. I'm looking forward to it."

Adam smiles with that open expression of his and nods to our left. Damn, we've already arrived at the Pump & Sip, our breakfast destination. It feels too soon. I was enjoying the peace of our run with the sounds of the wind gusting through the leaves, the dogs' claws clicking on the pavement, and the deep rumble of Adam's voice as he'd talked.

This place is just as busy as it was the last time we swung by here. Through the gas station window I can see a crowd inside, and an electronic bell chimes every few seconds as patrons come and go. The atmosphere is far too chaotic for the dogs, so we loop their leashes around a small tree, leaving them secure and together. Then Adam pulls the door open, and we step inside the unassuming gas station.

Wow.

The place is packed, with a line of people snaking from the counter to the far wall and then looping around the perimeter of the room to the door we just entered. Last I checked, this town isn't that big. Where did all these people come from? Is this the entire town, or does the throng include travelers passing through on the highway too?

"Probie," Adam says from beside me. I'm confused by the word until I see that Adam is speaking to someone else as he asks, "What are you doing up this early on your day off?"

Standing a few customers ahead of us in line, a hulking beefcake of a man turns around and glances between Adam and me, then smiles widely when he answers, "There's never a day off when your dad runs a construction company."

How do these two know each other? I watch their body language, trying to translate the energy between them. They're friendly, but guarded. Familiar, yet distant. Did they date?

After a moment where all of us smile awkwardly at each other, the hulk—who's built like a Cross Fit dude who flips tractor tires as part of his workout—gives up his spot in line to join us at ours. "Hi," he says to me. "I'm Knox County."

Knox County? What a name. Momentarily forgetting my manners, I just stare at him. Then I remember to speak and say, "I'm Markus Ely. Nice to meet you."

We shake hands, and despite the guy's massive bulk and the weird energy between him and Adam, his handshake is firm but very friendly.

"Ely, right, you're the town's new vet. I've been hearing all about you from Dee. Something about a wedding invite."

I chuckle, still surprised by how gossipy everyone is in this town. Most of my life I've lived in places that people called "small," but those towns had tens of thousands or hundreds of thousands of residents. Krause has just over fifteen hundred souls—half the size of your average cruise ship. This is *truly* a small town, and it seems everyone here already knows something about me. While I know nothing about them.

Like he can sense the discomfort that fact gives me, Adam says, "Markus, Knox is the new probationary officer at my fire station."

Aha! They're colleagues. Not lovers. Why that thought sends a tidal wave of relief through me, I will not analyze right now… Or maybe I will. Because this encounter has me wondering a few things: Is Adam out? Am I? I was out at A&M, but this town is a blank slate. What do I want my first mark to be? And if I'm out, am I out *with* Adam? This is our second very public meal together… Does that mean that *we* are together—

"What about you guys? Why are you out so early this morning?" Knox asks.

His use of "you guys" makes it sound like we're together, a unit, and when he asks why we're "out," I get a little shiver up my spine. Does Adam hear it, too, and does he like what he hears?

In answer to Knox's spoken questions and my silent ones, Adam says, "Markus and I kept running into each other when we were jogging with our dogs, so I figured I'd show him around town, come to where the locals get their grub."

Hmm. That doesn't sound very *together*.

Fortunately, the food line moves fast at the Pump & Sip, and before I can put too much thought to it, we're at the counter.

Knox orders so much food I think he'll clean the place out, but the two women manning the counter bring out more trays, the piping hot pastries leaving a trail of steam and drooling customers in their wake.

They pack up his order in a couple of bags, and Knox gives us a nod as he carries his breakfast haul out to his truck, destined for one of the new housing developments over on the highway.

Finally, it's our turn. My eyes widen, and my mouth waters as I stare at all the goodies in the glass case, but I let Adam order for both of us, curious what he likes. He orders a few of the sausage, cheese, and jalapeño klobasneks as well as cream cheese kolaches for dessert.

The women behind the counter work efficiently, one stuffing the food into a bag as the other brings us bottles of water and rings us up. This time I insist on paying, and when we're set, I carry the food while Adam handles the waters, and we head out to the dogs.

A chilly gust of wind tries to pull the door off its hinges, and I push it closed behind me as the stormfront blows through the street, whipping leaves off the trees and blasting us with plumes of road dust. The sky darkened to a dusky gloom while we were inside, and deep rumbles of approaching thunder have Drusilla whining anxiously.

"The rain won't be long now. Come on, let's run for cover," Adam says as we unfasten the dog leashes from the tree.

He gestures toward Main Street, then he and Drusilla sprint in that direction. Rufus and I follow, the pace pushing me past the point of exhaustion. But it feels good, my muscles straining forward as the cold, damp air tries to push me back.

In the end, we can't outrun the storm. The rain catches us as we turn onto Main Street. Ahead, the main square gazebo stands as a beacon, a dry shelter from the torrent falling from the sky. We pick up our pace, racing to the structure and taking the steps two at a time.

Finally sheltered from the storm, I bend over, huffing in air, trying to catch my breath. When I can, I stand again and push the soaked strands of hair out of my face. Adam paces in a little circle, his fingers laced behind his head, catching his breath. His green shirt is soaked, turning it a darker color and painting it over every bulge and muscle in his chest and arms. And, speaking of bulges, his running shorts seem to show— No, wait, those are the bottles of water, shoved into his pockets. Which reminds me… I look at the damp paper bag in my own hand and worry that the storm might have ruined our food.

The driest spot beneath our shelter is the southeast corner, so I go there, squatting to set the bag down and look inside. The food seems safe, dry, and intact, and the smell attracts everyone else. Adam and I shoo the dogs away as we divvy up the food and beverages, then we sit there on the cool cement floor of the old bandstand to eat our break-fast together.

I start with my dessert first, as usual, sinking my teeth into the soft sugary pastry with a warm dollop of cream cheese at the top, and I damn near die and go to heaven. Adam smiles and nods at the delighted noises I make as I devour the treat. It's delicious, and when I've finished, I lick my fingers clean of the sweetness.

Next, I reach into the bag for my serving of savory. I've had kolaches before, but this is my first klobasnek. It looks like an ordinary bread roll, but the moment I bite into it, I know it's like nothing I've eaten before. Inside the roll is a link of kielbasa sausage nestled in a cushion of melted cheddar cheese. A couple slices of jalapeño pepper add the perfect kick.

"Ohmygod!" I exclaim rudely, because my mouth is completely full of food. But really, "Ohmyfuckinggod!"

Adam laughs, seeming to delight in watching me savor the rest of my klobasnek as he enjoys his kolache. And right then, in that moment, everything seems perfect and good and nice and easy. The sensation—what is this, peace?—feels foreign to me.

So, of course, I ruin it when I say, "I wouldn't be so naïve as to say this is the best thing I've ever had in my mouth, but it's damn close."

Adam blinks at me, then bursts into a fit of laughter. The acoustics of the bandstand and the raging storm around us amplify the sound, filling my ears and heart and soul. "Well, now I need to know what tops that list."

I raise a brow, but don't take the bait. This is not the time to talk about the myriad of things I've had in my mouth. Instead, I watch the storm.

Rain falls in torrents that drum loudly on the gazebo's metal roof. Lightning fingers across the sky, and thunder rumbles ominously. Gusts of wind shed the trees of their leaves and a few branches too. And the temperature has dropped at least twenty degrees in the last ten minutes.

This isn't just some drippy little rain shower. It's a Blue Norther, a storm fueled by Canada-cold fury that explodes with violence when it meets the steamy moisture of the Gulf of Mexico. It seems odd, to feel such peace in the heart of a raging tempest, but as I glance over at Adam and the dogs, peace is the word that keeps coming to mind.

"Don't you just love storms like this?" Adam asks as he wipes his hands and stuffs his trash into the empty sack. He grins over at me, then stretches his legs out as he lies on his back. Staring up at the vaulted ceiling of the bandstand and the raging storm at its edges, he adds, "So much energy and excitement in the air. So much…fucking…*passion*."

Hmm. Where I feel peace, he feels passion. Interesting.

CHAPTER 8
ADAM

"Cock-a-doodle-doo! Hello! Hello! Hello! This is your number one favorite queer fireman Rooster Crows, coming at you live from—weirdly enough—a wedding!" I turn the camera on my phone around to show viewers the rows of seats filling up with wedding guests in anticipation of the big event. Bringing the camera back to me, I wrap my arm around Drew's shoulders, tugging him into the shot with me as I rave about him. "Can you believe it? My boy here is getting hitched! I could not be more happy for him and his lovely lady, and I promised them I wouldn't stream the entire ceremony, so I'll be popping in from time to time to share my warm, fuzzy feelings tonight. Be sure to like, follow, and comment with your well wishes for our favorite groom. Ciao, my brood!"

I plant a kiss on Drew's cheek, and he laughs as he flattens his palm over my phone camera. "Okay, okay. Enough of that. I've got places to be."

I chuckle as I end the video and slip my phone into my pocket, turning my focus entirely on Drew for his big day. The guy is practically shaking with nerves. He keeps adjusting his tie, leaving it more askew each time. I push his hands away.

"I don't understand why you post so much of yourself on social media," Drew says as I fuss, getting the knot of his tie just right before adjusting his badge on the left breast of his jacket and straightening the medals on his right. "I could never be that open with strangers online."

I shrug. I've never been able to explain to myself or anyone else why I like to stream. It started out many years ago as a video diary, a place to share my thoughts about life, liberty, and the pursuit of happiness as a queer man in small-town Texas. Perhaps I was looking for my people, seeking a community going through the same drama I was. And hot damn, did I find that community. I have over two hundred thousand followers on my social channels, and views have been growing by leaps and bounds lately too. I've posted everything from videos of me cooking breakfast to late night confessional musings to my workouts. My workout videos are the crowd favorites. But the feedback I've received regarding my frank insights into life as a gay man in a conservative place have been the most meaningful.

Hearing from young men that I've helped them navigate their own challenges is what keeps me sharing. So I guess it's my contribution, my way to connect with a community that is so much larger than this small town. But instead of telling Drew all of that, I just go with, "It's therapeutic."

"For you or your viewers?"

I shrug again. "Both?"

He sniffs out a laugh, because my response doesn't answer a damn thing. But I change the subject when I clap my hands on his shoulders and ask a much better question: "You ready to get married?"

His expression turns serious as he takes a deep breath in and lets it out before answering, "Yes. Very ready."

I set Drew's Pershing cap on his head, then put my own on and lead the way out to the altar.

Drew and Chloe's backyard is dazzling. The sunlight sparkles as it sinks to the horizon in a spray of orange and gold. Twinkle lights are strewn through the trees and clusters of candles flicker atop boulders and rocks, giving this place an intimate feel despite the dozens of guests filling every square inch of available space.

I remember when this little hill was the location of the oldest homestead in the county, the old Krause family farm. When Chloe's grandma died and bequeathed it to her, she only planned to fix it up and sell it.

That was before everything changed, though. Before Chloe met Drew and the two of them became one, a unit. And it was before Chloe's piece-of-shit father burned the old house down with her still inside.

Fortunately, her dad only managed to kill himself with that fire, and from those ashes, Drew and Chloe built something truly beautiful —a rock-solid relationship as well as an exquisite house and this stunning backyard.

Chloe—a newly graduated architect with a degree from the University of Texas—designed it, and she and Drew brought in County Sons Construction to build it. The house is made of native stone and designed to complement the landscape rather than scar it. Plus, there's this stunning view of the hill country undulating in violet waves as the sun sets on a fine Saturday evening.

The arbor we built for the ceremony stands atop a small outcropping of limestone. It's draped with twinkle lights, giving it a warm glow as evening approaches. This is where Drew and I come to stand as we smile at the assembled crowd and wait for the blushing bride to make her entrance.

Chief Watson—who will officiate today—is the picture of patience, while the groom and I fidget. Drew fiddles with his jacket cuffs, like he needs something to hold onto until his bride finally joins him and he can clasp her hands.

The uniform chafes me, too, but I stand stoic as I set my hand on Drew's shoulder and whisper, "You've got this, Catman. No need to be nervous."

He chuckles a little. "Is it that obvious?"

The guy is practically shivering with anticipation, but pointing that out probably won't help. Watts comes to the rescue, leaning in to whisper some fatherly wisdom. "It's natural to be anxious, but trust me, the moment you see your bride walking down that aisle, you'll forget the rest of us are even here."

While Watts is talking to Drew, I take his wisdom to heart, too, and steal a glance at the reason I'm so nervous up here. Sitting on the left, about five rows back, Markus sports a slim-fit, charcoal-grey suit with black shirt and tie, and, God, he sports it *well*. With his hair combed neatly into a dark wave that highlights the sharp line of his jaw, and his light eyes shielded from the sun behind a pair of dark glasses, he is the very definition of debonair.

I can't stop stealing glances at him, but it's not fair that I can't see where he's looking behind those tinted lenses. Fortunately, the ceremony music starts, and everyone turns their attention toward the house.

Dee steps from the doorway in a satiny blue dress. I've never seen her in a dress before today. She looks like a 1940s bombshell with her blond hair down and curling around her shoulders. The wedding photographer—aka her fiancé, Rico—takes a whole lot of photos of her making her way to the altar to stand with us.

Now, it's time for everyone to turn their attention to the bride. We look to the back of the house, where a wall of windows glow with candles lit inside the living room. That's where Chloe takes the arm of her hero, retired Fire Chief Big Mac McKenna. The two of them step outside, and I think everyone here sighs a little at the sweet image of them. He first met Chloe when he rescued her as a child from a car accident, and since her return to Krause, he's become something of a father figure to her. It's only natural that he would walk her down the aisle.

But I didn't truly prepare myself for the sight of them—Big Mac in his dress blues, his chest covered in the medals of his many years of fire service, looking down so sweetly at the woman marrying into our fire family today.

Beside me, I hear Drew's breath hitch in his lungs at the sight of Chloe in her wedding dress. She's stunning in a soft chiffon sheath gown. The fabric flows around her like water as she and Big Mac start their walk up the aisle.

I glance over at our groom. His eyes are shining with unshed tears, and the sight brings a little tear to my own eyes. Drew, like Chloe, is an orphan. Our family is all he's ever had; except now, he has Chloe, and she has him, and damn there goes another tear. I've been lucky in my life to have a loving family, for the most part, a family who accepts me for who I am, and I rejoice in seeing this new family as it takes shape.

When Big Mac and Chloe reach the altar, he gives her hand to Drew and presses a sweet kiss to her forehead as he steps back to take a seat. And, now Chloe's eyes are wet with tears too.

Watts comes forward to start the proceedings. He's a deacon in his church, so they asked him to handle the wedding—even though it's not a religious ceremony—and Watts works his magic over the guests and the bride and groom. He tells a few funny stories of how the two met, how Drew fell so hard for her, and how we all had the privilege of watching.

When it comes time for the exchange of rings, Inez—Dee's future mother-in-law and Chloe and Drew's next door neighbor—herds Drew and Chloe's cats up from the front. Bodhi and Utah were chilling pretty comfortably as people gave them attention before the ceremony, but now they have an important job to do. Everyone coos and giggles over the cats in their adorable little bow ties, which Chloe and Drew bend down to untie so they can retrieve their wedding rings.

It's so freaking cute.

With a very sweet, tear-soaked exchange of vows, and some R-rated kissing, the deed is done. Our brother Drew is a married man, a husband to an amazing wife, and with that revelation, their kiss turns a little toward NC-17 as he scoops Chloe into his arms and devours her. Their guests hoot and holler.

As we, the wedding party, turn to the seated guests to join them in celebration, my focus zeros in on Markus. He took his sunglasses off for the ceremony, so finally I can follow his gaze. To my delight, his gaze is focused squarely on me.

CHAPTER 9

MARKUS

"Oh, goodness, you're Dr. Ely, the new vet, aren't you?" The voice comes from behind me, pulling my thoughts from where they've been focused all afternoon: on Adam. It pains me to look away from him, down at the woman who's speaking to me. She's in her sixties, I'd guess, and she gazes up at me with wide, twinkling eyes. "It's so wonderful to meet you. Did you enjoy the wedding?"

I open my mouth to answer, but before I can get a word out, she clasps her hand around my arm and hollers over my shoulder. "Rebecca, dear, come here."

Rebecca? Who's Rebecca? Glancing over, I see an attractive young woman in a red dress frowning at my conversation companion. When she hesitantly joins us, the older woman makes introductions. "This is my granddaughter Rebecca. She's a junior at Southwest Texas State studying marketing. Rebecca, this is *Doctor* Markus Ely. He's new to town, and he's a doctor!"

"Actually, I'm a veteri—"

"An animal *doctor*." Rebecca's grandma—who still hasn't told me her own name—clarifies, emphasizing that word.

Rebecca blinks at me. I blink at her. "Nice to meet you," we both say and shake hands.

Silence follows, but it's soon filled by Rebecca's grandma as she makes some excuse to leave us alone.

Chuckling, I ask Rebecca, "Does this happen to you a lot?"

"Yes." Rebecca grins. "Granny Newsom won't be happy until I have someone put a ring on my finger and a baby in my womb, and you are an animal *doctor*, so all the better."

I chuckle again but inwardly grimace at the idea that I'm an eligible bachelor in this small town, and that is likely the reason for all my invitations to weddings and picnics and bowling leagues.

"Sorry you've been saddled with this. Though, I am very pleased to meet you. It's wonderful to hear that Krause finally has a vet again. Doc Evans's retirement was a major hardship for this town. We're glad to have you. How are you fairing?"

Before I can answer her question, someone shoves a champagne glass into my hand and grabs my elbow, yanking me away from Rebecca. I grimace with apology as I'm dragged away, then glance at my captor.

It's Dee—the maid of honor and bride-to-be—looking lovely. Before I can ask why she's dragging me from one end of the reception tent to the other, she tells me, "Come meet the crew."

The crew? What crew? I have no idea what she's talking about, but I get a pretty good idea when she takes me to the wedding party table. Dee comes to a stop and waves her arm to indicate "the crew."

Drew and Chloe are in the center. He's sitting in a chair with the bride in his lap, carefully feeding her cake, none of that mash-it-into-her-face nonsense with this guy. The two are clearly in love, and it's enough to make my stomach somersault a little bit.

Beside them sits an attractive Hispanic man and the adorable little boy who visited the office for PB's and J's checkups. The boy plays with Bodhi and Utah and doesn't even notice me. Dee moves over to the man and introduces him—Rico, her fiancé and Mateo's father. Then Dee settles onto Rico's lap and waves a dismissive hand to her left as she says, "And of course, you already know Rooster."

Adam, the primary focus of my attention all afternoon, stares up at me from his seat. Candle light glows golden in his green eyes, and my God, it's stunning how truly handsome the man is.

All through the ceremony, my attention was riveted to him in his dress blues, white gloves, and Pershing cap. He looked so polished, like he shined. His cap is set aside with his gloves now, and his dark, curly red mohawk is braided, making him look—from the starched collar up—like some Viking marauder of yore.

The look he gives me now has marauder vibes, too, fierce and sexy and—

"Say something for the camera," Adam instructs, interrupting my lusty thoughts.

The camera? I frown as Adam turns his back to me. Only then do I notice that he's holding his phone to take video, and now he's framed us both in the same shot, me staring like an idiot over his shoulder.

"Uh...hi," I muster, lamely.

"Any well wishes for the happy couple?" Adam prods for more.

I look over at said happy couple, totally engrossed in each other. They have no idea I'm even here. Turning back to Adam and his camera phone, I push a smile onto my lips, raise my glass and say, "Cheers to a long and happy marriage."

"Hear! Hear!" Adam says. He and Dee and Rico all raise their glasses with me and we drink.

Adam turns his camera on himself as he takes a sip of champagne, then winks at the lens and says, "Ciao, my brood," before he presses a few buttons on the screen and sets it aside.

Ciao, my brood? What does that mean? I try to figure it out as I stand awkwardly in front of the table. Dee, seeming to sense my discomfort, leaves Rico's lap long enough to grab my elbow again and lead me to an empty chair beside Adam. "Sit!" she commands, like I'm a dog.

I frown, but Adam quickly joins Dee in offering me the seat. "Yes. Please, sit. My plus-one wandered off when the dancing started."

His plus one?

"She's the dancing queen, and none other shall reign supreme," he continues.

She. Worse than learning he brought a date to this wedding is learning the date is a woman. I could have sworn he was—

"Challenge accepted! There is only one dancing queen here, and I will hold onto that title if it's the last thing I do," Dee shouts at Adam and kisses Mateo's forehead as she steals his dad away to dance with her.

Adam hugs the little boy to him and makes some joke about his dad having two left feet. Then he turns to me. "This should be good. LT Dee is overly competitive on a normal day. Add alcohol and a dance-off, and we're in for a show."

The smile on Adam's face is so beautiful, it has me smiling too. "LTD?" I ask, just to keep him talking.

"LT Dee." He emphasizes the pause between the T and Dee. "We've been calling her that since Watts was promoted to Fire Chief and Dee took over as Lieutenant."

Suddenly, I want to know everything about his job, about his role on their team. "What's your title?"

"I'm the Driver Engineer." He smiles, and it's gorgeous, full of bright white teeth and bracketed by perfect dimples. Then, to my delight and astonishment, he sings, "I drive big trucks, and I cannot lie!" to the tune of "Baby Got Back," and I laugh. God, I like talking to this guy. He's **easy** to be around.

His smile widens, like he enjoys the sound of my laughter, and it feels like he's flirting. The look in his eyes feels like flirting too.

With a little shrug, he adds, "Though, technically, it's not a fire truck, it's a fire engine. Engine Thirty-One. But 'I drive big engines' doesn't have the same ring to it."

He's a little drunk; it's clear in the free and easy way he talks about himself in that deep rumbly voice. I want more. Want to shower him with champagne so he'll tell me in minute detail what the difference is between a fire truck and a fire engine.

But a slender redheaded woman with pretty eyes walks past me to drape her arms around Adam's neck and in a singsong voice coaxes, "Come dance with me, you big cock."

Oh. Kay. This must be his plus-one. I stand from her seat as Adam jokes that she's too drunk to dance, and she'll end up showing her underwear to half the town like the last wedding he took her to. She argues that's impossible because she's not wearing any underwear.

And *that's* my cue to leave. With a little wave to Adam, I indicate I'm heading for the food table, but that's a lie. I leave.

The appearance of Adam's panty-free date is, well, disappointing. Clearly I've been imagining things were heating up between me and Adam. The man is here with a woman. Is he even gay? I know I can be socially awkward at times, but generally I'm pretty good at reading cues and signals. How was I so wrong this time?

Tugging my tie loose, I make my way to my car, already imagining what a quiet night in with Rufus will be like.

Heaven.

CHAPTER 10
ADAM

"Can we please stop talking about my baby boy's cock at the breakfast table?" Mom says loudly, and everyone goes silent. Even the dogs out in the kennels seem to hush for a moment. But silence never lasts long in this house, and soon we're at it again.

This time, my sister Ava breaks the quiet, smirking at me as she clarifies, "I didn't say he *had* a big cock! I just called *him* a big cock! Like a rooster. Duh!"

My other sisters—Anna and Alice—turn practically purple as they try not to burst into laughter. Their husbands—Gary and Clint—focus on their food and just keep eating. This debate about me and my cock isn't anything unusual. The Newman family loves and laughs loud and hard, and we argue loud and hard too.

This isn't an argument though. Everyone knows Ava fucked up.

Between bites of Mom's famous Sunday-morning pancakes, I say, "Well, Markus's rapid exit from the wedding suggests he thought you were talking about *my* big cock."

A collective groan rises around the table because clearly, despite

Mom's request, my cock is absolutely the thing we're going to talk about at the breakfast table.

"And for that, I'm sorry." Ava finally relents, but then her face shifts, a scheming-sister glint in her eyes as she rubs her hands together. "How do we fix this?"

"Oh, no! No way! *We* won't do anything." I look around at my family, staring daggers at each of them. They stare back, and all the busybody energy they project is terrifying. "I want you *all* to stay out of it. This isn't a problem for the Newman women to solve."

Alice and Anna bust into a butchered variation of Vanilla Ice's lyric regarding problem solving. Their husbands chuckle, and I smirk. Ava isn't distracted. She pushes, trying to convince me to involve her in whatever my plan is to win Markus over. "But I caused the problem, so let me fix it."

"How exactly do you think you can fix this? Are you going to go up to a virtual stranger and say, 'Hey, just so you know, I'm his sister'? Do you think it's any better that my *sister* was my date to the wedding, and my *sister* couldn't stop talking about my cock? Do you think it will fix anything if you make us look like the living embodiment of a Welcome to Schitt's Creek sign?"

Despite my very valid rant, my family isn't listening. Ava turns to Mom, gushing, "Oh my God, Mom, you should have seen this guy. Absolute stunner! Dark hair with this surfy wave to it and eyes so blue you'd want to go for a swim. And he was making soft little puppy-dog eyes at our boy."

Mom rolls her eyes at my sister. "I met him, dear, when I took Elsa in for her vaccinations and—"

Ava keeps talking, directing her comments to the whole Newman brood now. "During the ceremony, I just happened to grab a seat on the row across from him, and I can tell you, his gaze was firmly frozen on our precious little cock the entire time."

"So now it's little?" I grumble.

"Not *it*, darling, *you*." Ava blows me a kiss. The "little" remark is a running joke with my sisters. I'm a foot taller and at least fifty pounds of pure muscle larger than any of them, but because I was born last, they delight in calling me their little brother.

I love these women. Absolutely, I do. But I've reached my limit for cock talk with them today. Besides, my shift starts in a couple of hours. Shoving a piece of bacon into my mouth, I stand to leave. With hugs and kisses all around, I make my way to the back door to grab Drusilla for a jog. My parting words are, "I love you all, but no one will fix anything with regard to Markus. There is nothing *broken* and therefore nothing for you busybodies to *fix*. Got it?"

Not a single one of them says "got it" back to me. They just stare blankly at me, like a flock of innocent little lambs. Groaning, I go, knowing that it's a waste of time to argue with them about staying out of my personal life. My family has been overly protective and all up in my business since the day I was born. Well, my father wasn't. But my mom and sisters have been protecting and babying me from the start. You'd think I'd be used to it by now.

Putting all the drama out of my head, I jog across the lawn to the dog kennels, where I find Drusilla wagging her little tail so hard her whole body wiggles. Aww, there is nothing quite like the simplicity of a dog's affection. I lavish the sweet girl with rubs and kisses, then we start our jog downtown.

With the weather mild and breezy, it's a great day for a run. When we reach Markus and Rufus's place, I climb the stairs and knock on the front door. No one answers.

I'm not entirely surprised. Today is Sunday, the one day a week that the veterinary clinic is closed. Perhaps Markus and Rufus are running errands, or they've gone into one of the bigger cities for a brunch break from small-town life. Regardless, they aren't here, and Drusilla shares my disappointment. We continue our run, just the two of us, going down along the path by the river, up around the high school, and back into downtown.

We stop at the main square, where I get Drusilla some water, then settle onto a bench and toss a ball for her while I check the latest interactions on the video I posted last night. There's been a lot of activity, with most people commenting about the hunk who stood awkwardly at my table, staring at me as I pointed my camera phone up at him.

"Oh, hello, who is this tall drink of water?" one commenter asked.

"Cheers to you, hot stuff, whoever you are," another added.

Many more ask for details: Is he a friend, a friend with benefits, or more? What's his name, why does he look so adorably awkward?

The comments are amusing, but I don't reply to any of them. I hadn't really considered what adding Markus's face to my online channels would mean. But when Rooster Crows features a hot guy on his social media, of course tongues will wag.

With a groan, I slip my phone away, toss the ball a few more times, then walk Drusilla back to Mom's place and head to the fire station to shower and change before my shift begins. The moment I step into the kitchen, I'm greeted by the amazing aroma of brewing coffee and a chorus of, "Hey, ya big cock!"

I've heard of the "Sunday Funday" concept, but I've never had the luxury of partaking. Well, that's not entirely true. It's not that I'm denied the luxury of weekends; I simply opt not to use that time for relaxation. In general, I'm not the sort of person who wanders aimlessly or sits still. I aim, and I achieve. Relaxing has always just seemed like a waste of time to me.

If I had my druthers, I wouldn't close the clinic on Sundays, but this is a small town with more churches than pets. Folks around Krause wouldn't take too kindly to a veterinarian who doesn't observe the Sabbath. So I have Sundays off.

While I could certainly use a day of rest each week, the reality is that Sunday is the only day I have to run errands. And that's the plan for today. I sleep in a little later than usual, and instead of going for a morning jog, I get Rufus into the car, and we take a drive down to San Antonio. Rumor has it there's an office furniture outlet there with great deals. Today's task is to upgrade the clinic waiting-area furniture with something from this century.

The drive is lovely. Fall in Texas is not much to speak of. We don't get "leafers" looking for the riot of changing colors like you get up north. Here in Texas, the Red Oak leaves go red, and the rest of the leaves turn yellowish brown then fall off.

Still, the fall's lower temperatures are a welcome relief after the kiln-like heat of summer. Today, it's not supposed to get much warmer than the mid-eighties, and it feels fantastic. I roll the windows down in my car and take a windy two-lane route south.

Once we're in the San Antonio metro area, the roads widen and clog with cars, and I use my navigation app to find our destination. The furniture outlet is in a wide, squatty building surrounded by an empty blacktop parking lot. On the door, a sign indicates that the furniture store, too, is closed on Sundays.

Okay. Change of plans. Guess it will be a Sunday Funday after all.

As quickly as we entered the big city, we leave it, taking rural roads northwest to explore the area, aiming in the general direction of Krause. Along the way, I find a fast food restaurant with a drive through and get some food, but I wait until we find a secluded turnoff before I stop to eat.

In the shade of a tall cottonwood tree, on the bank of a shallow creek, I eat my food while Rufus sniffs the water's edge. A few bluegill fish eye him suspiciously from between rocks and reeds, occasionally splashing at him when he gets too curious. The dog hops backward, huffing with annoyance, and I chuckle.

It's nice, just sitting here with nothing to do and nowhere to be. We should do this Sunday Funday thing more often.

Though, the slow pace has done little to keep my mind off last night's wedding revelations. "Come dance with me, you big cock," has been on repeat all day—an earworm without a tempo—and memories of that bouncy little redhead who draped herself across Adam's shoulders like a fur stole lives rent free in my mind too. I try distracting myself, chatting with Rufus and skipping rocks across the creek, but it's much too quiet to drown out all this noise in my head.

In the few weeks I've known Adam, I've formed an image of him in my mind, and in that image, he was gay. Apparently I was wrong, and the man I've been crushing on since I first laid eyes on him is completely unavailable to me. That's nothing new. Plenty of the men

I've crushed on have been straight. Though I don't recall any straight strangers ever being as friendly as Adam. He's given me jogging tours of the town. Taken me out for breakfast...twice. It really felt like something.

Enough! I need to stop fixating. It is what it is. He is who he is. And I am who I am, and if friendship is the extent of the relationship that can form between us, that's okay. Really. It has to be. I like him too much to kick him out of my life just because I can't get him into my bed.

So, enough! Enough fixating on him. Enough avoiding him. The day is growing long, and I need to get back home to balance the books and review my schedule for Monday.

With a heavy sigh—one that earns me a glance and a sympathetic whine from Rufus—I stand and wipe dirt off the back of my jeans, then call to him. "Rufus, let's go home, buddy."

Rufus hops a few times, excited to be moving again, and jumps right into the back seat of the car, sitting very prim and still so I can snap him into his safety harness. Then I slide into my seat behind the wheel, fasten my seatbelt, and—

That's all I remember.

No, that's not true. Glimpses, watercolor images, shatter into shards of broken memories. The screech of tires, the crunch of metal, the pain, the sudden panic.

Now, everything is silent. No, not silent, muffled.

As I try to focus on the noise, so many sounds come at me at once, like a new collision, a deafening cacophony. There is a high-pitched squeal that rings in my ear, and it's punctuated with bursts of noise, like loud bangs. No, not bangs, barks.

Rufus.

He was with me. We were together in the car. There's been an accident. Where is he now? Is he hurt?

My disorientation dissolves, my focus sharpening as I push through the confusion that blocks my view like wisps of smoke. No. Wait. That's…the airbag.

I shift and move the fabric out of my face. Some of the deafening sound ceases too. I've been pressing on the horn. Now as I move, the shrill screeching stops. But other noises fill the void. More screeching comes from elsewhere, and closer…there it is again, that harried, frantic…barking.

Rufus!

Without the airbag clouding my vision, I focus and take in the disorienting images of my car, broken and wrapped all around me. There's something wet on me, in my hair, on my face. And to my right, Rufus is whining and barking and moving around.

I turn to look into the back seat but yelp and wince as pain lances through my neck and down my spine.

Fuck.

But… Rufus. I need to see him, see that he's okay. God, please let him be okay.

Slowly this time, I turn around just enough to see Rufus in the back seat, right where I left him. The seat belt strap I used to secure him has done its job. Though clearly upset—barking even louder now that he's roused me, and I've turned to catch his gaze—he appears to be unharmed.

Feeling better about at least that little bit in this chaotic moment, I turn back to the front of the car, trying to see what happened elsewhere.

That's when I notice the other vehicle—a bright orange Kia crumpled into mine where my passenger-side front end would normally be. And this close, I can see through the windshield and into the other car. Someone is bent over the steering wheel, not moving.

"Hello?" I holler, but my voice comes out rough and so quiet it's barely a whisper. Clearing my throat, I try again, really yelling this time. "Hello?"

My throat feels cracked and shredded, like I've gargled with broken glass. But the windshield is intact, no glass to gargle with. Regardless, I'm not doing much good just sitting here yelling toward someone in another car. Instantly, my head clears, and my thoughts snap into order: I need to help.

With shaky fingers, I struggle to unfasten my seat belt, then fumble more when it comes to opening my door. Placing one foot onto the ground and then the other, I wobble. This is what I imagine a moonwalk would feel like, bouncy and unsteady.

Before anything else, I turn to my back door and open it. Rufus is anxious, whining as he whacks his tail against the seat and tugs at his restraint, clearly frustrated with being strapped into a broken vehicle.

Everything hurts as I lean in to unfasten him, and he whines as he licks all over my face, clearly happy to have me near. When I manage to unclasp his harness from the car, he practically pushes me backward out the door so he can escape. Stumbling, I struggle to recover my balance as he jumps down and swings around in a circle like he's taking in the scene.

With him safe and freed from the wreckage, I walk quickly around the back end of my car to the driver's window of the other vehicle. My shaky fingers fumble at my pocket, but I manage to pull my phone out.

Quickly, I call 911. When they answer, I explain about the accident and try to determine where we are so they can find us. As I talk, I approach the other car. The driver's window is shattered, glass sparkling on the pavement all around. I command Rufus to sit and stay away from the wreckage. He's a very good boy, whining but following the command.

The person inside the car is leaning over the steering wheel, so I can't see their face, but I think it's Mildred Koenig, the town's librarian. I can't be certain, but I can't imagine anyone else around here drives a neon orange Kia. She doesn't respond to my voice as I call to her. She doesn't move at all.

I touch her neck, feeling for a pulse, holding my breath until… There! Like butterfly wings against my fingertips, it's just a flutter, but it's there. Relief washes over me as I count the beats and relay her pulse to the dispatcher. The woman on the other end assures me emergency responders are on the way, then she asks about my own condition.

"I'm fine," I tell the dispatcher as I switch to speakerphone, set it on top of the wrecked car, and try to pry the door open. The metal is bent and twisted and doesn't budge. So I do the best I can to comfort the woman through the window.

Gently brushing some of her hair aside, I finally get a good look at her. As I suspected, it's Mildred, the chatty librarian I've met a couple of times. Early on, she learned I love ghost stories, and apparently she loves telling them, because—

Suddenly, Mildred gasps and straightens in her seat, silencing the car's horn at the same time that she scares the ever-loving shit out of me. I stumble backward, nearly falling onto my ass on the glass and other wreckage littering the pavement.

Rufus barks. The woman at the 911 dispatch center must hear my scream because she asks a whole string of questions about what's going on and if we're okay. But my focus is fixed on Mildred, watching her blink and frown at the destruction.

"Mrs. Koenig, are you okay? Can you hear me?" I ask her as I return to her window, angling my head so I can get a better look at her face. She looks dazed, but uninjured.

"Try not to move too much. The ambulance is on its way, so just sit tight."

Mildred grimaces at me and squints to see where we are on the narrow county road. We're right in the middle, blocking both lanes of traffic. And with the afternoon sun casting long shadows through the trees, I imagine it would be difficult for another driver to see us. If someone were to come upon us, would they see us in time to stop, or would they run right into the wreck? Should I pull Mildred out, just in case?

Before I can fret too much, I hear the sweet siren song of rescue.

We're saved—Mildred, Rufus, and me. The shiny red fire truck grows larger as it nears us, and my relief grows with it. The driver stops abruptly about twenty feet away, angling to block the road, and sets the vehicle in park with the hiss of hydraulic brakes.

Several doors swing open at once, and legs encased in yellow pants hit the pavement. Then, from behind the driver's door, he appears: *Adam.*

My breath hitches in my lungs at the sight of him. My savior isn't just any ordinary hot firefighter, he's *the* hot firefighter I've been thinking about nonstop since I first laid eyes on him. And now, here he comes to save the day.

Christ almighty, he looks so…heroic…and *gorgeous*.

"Markus, are you okay?" Adam asks as he approaches. Before I can answer, he lifts his hands to palm my cheeks. This is our first touch—outside of the few cordial handshakes we've shared—and the sensation jolts awareness through my body. He's devastatingly gentle as he cradles my face between his blue palms and looks determinedly at my head, pulling my eyelids up to look deep into my eyes.

Wait. Blue? Why are his hands blue? I angle my chin to get a better look and realize he's wearing sterile gloves as he inspects me for injury.

Oh. Right. The wreck. I'd nearly forgotten.

"I… Uh. I'm fine, never better. I'm more worried about Mildred's neck," I say as I push his hands away and try to direct his attention to the woman who really needs his help.

Adam doesn't say anything, and Drew, the newlywed groom who passes us alongside Knox, tells me, "Don't you worry. We've got her."

"Shouldn't he be on his honeymoon?" I ask Adam as he puts his gentle blue hands on my shoulders and moves me away from the cars, toward an ambulance. When did that arrive? I glance around to see that two ambulances and two fire trucks are here now. One man in firefighter pants snaps flares open to set on the road, while a couple of others pull gear off the closest vehicle. Dee stands to the side, speaking into a CB radio.

Adam moves me to the shoulder of the road, where Rufus presses his full body against my shins like he needs to lean on me.

Or…

Maybe I need to lean on him…

And that's my last thought before lights out, last call, closing time.

No, wait, that's not right. My last coherent thought isn't about Rufus—it's about Adam. I hear him speak, that intoxicating rumble in his low voice as he says, "I've got you, Markus. You're going to be okay."

CHAPTER 12
ADAM

"Never better?" I grumble and catch Markus when he passes out. Christ, he's heavy, like a full metric ton of dead weight hanging from my arms.

I knew he was big. I've watched the way his muscles stretch and bunch when we run together. I've imagined those muscles stretching and bunching as he moves against me, beneath me, more than once. But right now—with all his weight hanging from my shoulders as I try to hold him up so his knees don't hit the ground—he's really fucking heavy.

Fortunately, the ambulance was right on our ass as we arrived on scene, and the first crew has a stretcher out and is rolling it my way. With a little help from Jared and Mason, the paramedics, we manage to get Markus onto his back on the stretcher so they can assess his condition.

He's bleeding profusely from a cut on his forehead, and I don't think he even realized he was injured. Ah, the power of adrenaline. But when he saw me, all of his energy drained, causing him to collapse. I'm just glad I was here to catch him.

Now, EMS stabilize his c-spine and record his vitals as they assess his head injury. He'll probably need a few stitches, nothing terribly bad given his strong pulse and respiration, but head wounds are tricky, and they bleed a lot. And Markus's injury is one hell of a gusher.

As the paramedics secure him to the gurney and get an IV line started, I know I still have a job to do here. I can't just stand around worrying about Markus anymore.

Turning my attention back to the scene, I remove my soiled gloves and pull on a clean pair as I approach the tangled wreckage. I easily recognize the other driver of the accident from her car. Mildred is the only person within thirty miles of this town who drives a bright orange Kia.

Sure enough, as I get closer to the driver's side, I see Mildred behind the wheel. She's a chatty woman, and the accident doesn't seem to have adversely affected that. She's peppering my team with questions as Probie pries a gap into the door seam at the hinges with a Halligan bar, and Drew maneuvers a hydraulic spreader into place to force the door out of our way.

Dee has stabilized Mildred's neck—despite the woman's protests that she's "perfectly fine"—and outfitted the librarian with safety goggles and a light blanket to keep the glass and other debris off her as Drew starts the machine.

Metal twists and groans, and the spreader roars with power as the car door curls back like the lid on a sardine can. Drew stops for a moment while Probie ties off a rope to the top of the door. When Drew starts the spreader again, Probie keeps tension on the rope, pulling the crumpling metal away from the passenger compartment.

Since they seem to have that task well covered, I turn my attention to Rufus. The poor dog is clearly upset by everything that's happened on this stretch of county road. Usually, he wags his tail furiously when I approach him—though it could be because he usually sees me accompanied by his favorite girl, Drusilla.

Now, however, he stands at the side of the road, pacing and whining and huffing at the chaotic scene. His tail is tucked between his legs, and his ears lie flat on his head. He doesn't bear his teeth or growl at me, but he does anxiously lick his chops a few times as he watches me approach.

I don't bother to put on my new gloves, instead stuffing them into my pocket. Watching him, too, I move slowly, angling my body and my gaze so I don't come at him with any aggressive energy. When I'm close but not looming over him, I stop and quietly speak in a calm, kind tone. "Hey, Rufus. How are you doing, buddy?"

Slowly, Rufus takes a step toward me, sniffing at one of my hands, then he sits down in front of me. I take that as an invite to pet him, so I crouch and give him some love, gently massaging his neck and chest. He sniffs and licks my arm, and I give him both of my hands, really massaging him now. "That's a good boy, Rufus. You're okay, aren't you? And your dad's going to be okay too. We're going to take good care of him for you."

Rufus leans his head into my palm, finally seeming to relax his posture so I can scratch him behind the ears. When he lets out a sweet little sigh, I completely fucking melt for the gentle giant. My presence in this stressful situation seems to soothe him, and his trust is truly humbling.

Over Rufus's head, I wave a hand in the air to get the attention of Mason, who's packing up some of the compartments on his ambulance rig. I holler for him to bring water and something for Rufus to drink from. He quickly comes to us with a water bottle and pours its contents into an emesis basin. We both pet Rufus for a moment while he sloppily laps up the water with his big tongue.

"Any injuries on him?" Mason asks.

"Not that I can see, but I'm going to call my mom to take him in at her refuge for the night. She can give him a full once-over. I'm worried about his paws with the glass on the pavement."

With a nod, Mason crouches and makes nice with Rufus before gently lifting and feeling the pads of his paws. The dog seems calm now, never nipping or yelping, and there's no blood on his feet, a small miracle considering the state of this road.

My sister Ava pulls up in her sheriff's deputy cruiser, and she agrees to let Rufus sit in her back seat while she works the scene. Later, she'll take him over to Mom's to board. When the dog is safe and secure, I step away from the noise of the running rigs to call my mom and let her know the plan.

"How's my boy?"

I can't help but grin at her usual greeting to me. "I'm good, Mom, but I need a favor."

I haven't even finished explaining the situation when she agrees and starts hollering at my brother-in-law Clint to prep a kennel for a last-minute guest.

Time is like taffy. It stretches and stretches and stretches some more. I've never had such a long shift. Not that it's actually longer than any of my other twenty-four-hour shifts, but this time I have somewhere else I need to be: the hospital.

We haven't had a callout since Mildred and Markus's collision on Route 10, so I've sat around the station, fretting and worrying and twiddling my thumbs. I'm desperate to know how Markus is doing, but the nurse on duty isn't telling me anything, and after my fifth call last night, she asked me, quite sternly, to stop calling every twenty minutes. And so, time has stretched all out of shape as I wait none too patiently.

Just after noon, the moment the chauffer for C shift turns up to relieve me from duty, I'm in my truck and racing over to the hospital. Once parked, I hustle inside, aiming for the front desk but take a quick detour into the gift shop for something to bring with me. Mom taught me never to arrive at a hospital room empty-handed, so I buy a stuffed animal. It's a little yellow labrador wearing a white lab coat, and there's a Get Well Soon balloon tied to its leg. The balloon bobs through the air as I return to the front desk to get directions to Markus's room.

"I'm sorry, but there's no patient here by that name," says the woman at the desk.

"What do you mean he's not here? I was on scene at the accident.

Jared and Mason indicated they were bringing him and Mildred here." I irritably shove the perky balloon out of my face as I lean over the desk, trying to get a glimpse of the nurse's computer screen over the counter.

She frowns at me and angles her monitor away, but taking a bit of pity on me she shares, "He checked out last night at about midnight."

He checked out? At midnight? That was twelve hours ago. He's been alone for twelve hours? "He has a concussion. Why would you let him leave?"

Her expression speaks volumes without saying a word, and instantly I know: he checked himself out against medical advice. Of course they would never have advised he leave their care so soon after a head injury. That stubborn—

"Son of a bitch!" I shout far too loudly and wince with apology at the nurse and the few people sitting in the lobby. Turning on my heels, I march out of the hospital. The Get Well Soon balloon bounces with my stride as I go to my truck, toss the plush puppy into the passenger seat, and aim for downtown, to the apartment above the vet clinic.

CHAPTER 13
MARKUS

My head is pounding. No, wait, that's the front door. And the noise won't stop.

Bang. Bang. Bang…

Bang. Bang. Bang.

Why is someone beating on my door? I climb off the couch, awkwardly balancing on weak legs. Everything hurts. It feels like every inch of me, both inside and out, is bruised and broken.

I shuffle to the door, and that incessant banging continues the whole way. When I'm finally there, having journeyed the long distance of ten feet, I struggle with the dead bolt and open it before remembering to check who it is first. Not smart, but I'm not thinking clearly.

The instant I crack open the door, it's pushed wider. Someone shoves a stuffed animal into my chest, and a Mylar balloon bounces against my face. I stumble backward with surprise and confusion, and when the balloon clears away from my vision, I stare down at a little stuffed lab dog in a lab coat. Squinting, I read the words printed on the lab's lab coat: "Trust me I'm a dog-tor."

It's cute. I chuckle. But my good humor only lasts a moment before I'm shocked back to reality with the harsh sound of an angry voice asking, "What the fuck is wrong with you?"

I look up. Pain lances through my neck and down my spine. Adam stands in my kitchen, frowning. He looks at once too large for this cramped apartment but also just right standing here in my space. And he's hot as hell in a FIRE T-shirt that stretches taught across his sculpted chest and big bulging biceps—

"Seriously, Markus, what the fuck?"

My name. He said my name. Tearing my ogling gaze away from his body, I see fire in his eyes, but it's not the *good* kind of fire. He's angry. At me.

"What?" I ask dumbly.

"Why would you check yourself out of the hospital?" Adam asks in a loud, demanding voice.

I grimace at his tone and pause to collect my thoughts. But all I can manage to say is, "I… Uh… I'm fine."

"Bullshit, you have a fucking concussion!" The volume of his voice hurts, his words slicing through my brain like they're punctuating his sentence with a big, sharp, spiky exclamation point.

I'm too tired to keep standing here, so I turn my back on Adam, hug the stuffed dog-tor to my chest, and shuffle to the kitchen table.

It takes me an inordinate amount of time to make it to one of the chairs there, and I struggle to pull it out. Soon, Adam is beside me, shifting the chair so I can sit. Grateful for the help, I grin at him, catching his eyes and holding his silent stare for just a moment before I carefully sit.

Once I'm settled, Adam pulls the opposite chair away from the table. I think he's going to take a seat, too, but instead he dumps a big, red canvas bag there, the words FIRE 31 NEWMAN spray-painted across the side with a stencil.

Rummaging around, he comes up with a blood pressure cuff, and I let him fit it over my bicep, silently staring at the curl of his eyelashes as he pumps the cuff and watches the dial. When that's finished, he finds another tool from his bag and brings it to me. I'm too focused on the feel of his hand on my face to notice what it is.

His touch is firm but gentle, and his eyes are gentler still as he tilts my chin up to face him, and—

"Ouch! What are you doing?" I yelp and wince and force my eyes shut as bright light floods my left eye. Even with my eyes closed, I see a delta of veins painted in neon colors on the backs of my eyelids.

"I'm checking your pupil response. Now open your eyes."

"But—"

"No buts." He huffs, sounding very exasperated with me. "I'm not fucking around with this, Markus. You have a concussion. You shouldn't have checked yourself out of the hospital. And you shouldn't be alone right now. So let me just make sure you don't have a serious brain injury, okay?"

Well, when he puts it like that… I blink my eyes open, squinting a little with fear of that blindingly bright light. This time, though, it doesn't hurt as much when he slashes the light across my gaze. I stare past the bright pinprick and focus on him, on those incredibly long, curly lashes and the depths of his gorgeous green eyes.

"What's my name?"

His question snaps me out of my ogling perusal. "Uh… Adam."

"What's your name?"

I huff, but his expression brooks no argument. "Markus."

"Where are we?"

"My kitchen."

"What day is it?"

"Sunday," I answer quickly, but the expression on his face sinks with concern, and I realize my mistake. Right, the sun has set and risen again since the car accident. "Monday."

Adam nods, puts the penlight back in his bag, and settles into the chair across from me as he keeps up the inquisition. "Do you have a headache?"

I shrug and nod, and even that bit of movement hurts.

"Why do you have a headache?"

"Because Mildred hit me with her car. How is she, by the way?"

"She's in stable condition at the hospital, *where you should be.*" He raises a brow like he's chastising a very naughty boy. And if he still had that pulse oximeter on my finger, he'd likely notice a change in my heart rate at the thoughts he's putting in my head. Changing the subject, he asks, "What's your favorite food?"

"Seriously?"

"Yes. Seriously."

"German chocolate cake."

"What's your favorite song?"

Huh? I'm so confused. "How does answering that help you diagnose a head injury?"

He grins with half of his mouth, and it's mesmerizing. "It doesn't. I'm just curious."

God, that smile is charming, disarming. That smile is dangerous. And it makes me smile, too, feeling a bit bashful with all his attention focused on me.

"Why'd you check yourself out of the hospital?" he asks next.

My smile sinks and so does Adam's.

After a moment, he tells me, "You hit your head in the accident, hard enough to cut it. That's stitched up, but swelling on your brain remains a concern. It's not safe for you to be alone for the next"—he checks his watch—"twelve hours or so."

His words send a chill through me. The doctors at the hospital had said pretty much the same thing, trying to frighten me into staying with tales of hypothetical hemorrhages on my brain and the depressing prospect of dying alone in my apartment.

"So I'm going to stay and keep an eye on you."

Uh…what?

"Have you eaten?" He changes the subject and doesn't wait for an answer. Assuming, correctly that I haven't, he stands and crosses to my fridge, opening it and poking around.

I look down at the plush puppy dog in my hands and feel a warmth in my chest as I realize how sweet this gift truly is. Adam went to see me in the hospital—brought me a get-well puppy—only to find me gone. So he came here.

And now, he's feeding me, taking care of me. He's clearly frustrated with my early release from the hospital, but it's plain to see his anger is defensive, a mask he wears to hide his worry. I can't remember the last time anyone worried about me, took care of me. I've been looking out for myself since I was fifteen, so his concern feels strange. Nice, but strange.

I grin at his back, charmed by his brusque display of affection, and finally answer one of his questions from before. "One More Try."

He pauses in all his slicing and dicing to look over his shoulder at me. "What?"

"My favorite song is George Michael's 'One More Try.' "

He stares at me for a long moment, then slowly he smiles and nods. "Good song."

When he returns his attention to cooking, it's my turn to ask questions—well, one question: "Where's Rufus?"

Adam doesn't spare me a glance this time as he answers, "He's at my mom's kennel, hanging out with Drusilla. We looked him over last night, and incredibly, he came through without a scratch."

A wave of intense relief washes over me. I'd suspected Rufus would be safe in Adam's care—certain that Adam would get Rufus off the shoulder of that road last night—but hearing him say it sets every nerve in my body to rest. Adam rescued me yesterday. And then he rescued my dog.

I stare at him, his strong shoulders shifting and pulling the fabric of his shirt taut as he cuts and stirs, his pants hugging his ass so nicely as he squats to dig a skillet out of a cupboard and stands again to turn on one of the stove's burners.

The warmth I feel for Adam in this moment is big and strange and great. But there's an emptiness too. Petting this stuffed animal is soothing, but it's not enough. I need Rufus here with me, so I can see with my own eyes that he's safe.

Like he can read my thoughts, Adam says, "I'll have someone bring him over if you're ready to see him. He won't jump on you, will he?"

I shake my head. "No, he's a good boy."

Adam grins at me over his shoulder, then he looks down at the stuffed dog I still have in my hands. His smile turns a little thoughtful as he goes back to cooking, but he uses one hand to pull his phone out of his pocket. I listen as he tells someone to bring Rufus over and gives my address as "above the vet clinic."

Once that's done, he turns his full attention to frying eggs and toasting bread. I stare at his ass, ogling like a creep as I stroke my puppy. That thought makes me laugh. As if "stroking my puppy" is a euphemism, and honestly, with the way Adam looks in those pants, it could be.

Adam glances at me. "Something funny?"

I could answer, but I don't. Instead, I go back to his unanswered question from earlier. "I checked myself out early because I hate hospitals. Had a…bad experience." I practically shiver at the cold memories flooding my mind, then try to shake them off. "Anyway, I just don't like them."

Adam's hands stop moving, and he glances at me, then he turns back to the stove to dish up our food. He brings two plates to the table, and it's a breakfast feast of eggs scrambled with cheese and diced veggies, toast with honey, and orange juice.

Using the fork he hands me, I shovel food into my mouth so fast I nearly choke, then wash it down with juice and pause to catch my breath. Clearly, I'm famished, considering I haven't eaten since my road trip with Rufus yesterday.

"Slow down, now. Those eggs aren't gonna run away from you."

That makes me laugh a little and gets me to slow as I continue to eat.

"What happened to make you hate hospitals?" Adam asks after a moment.

I finish my eggs, blot my lips on a napkin, and take a deep breath in, then let it out. *Here we go.* "I'm gay."

Adam's brows hit his hairline, and he chuckles a little before he says, "Me too."

Wait. What? "Really?"

"Yeah, the woman at the wedding was my sister."

Uh…

"Anyway you were saying…about hospitals."

Right. That. With another deep breath in and out, I just say it, spill it all. "When I was fifteen my parents found me making out with a friend from the football team. They're very conservative and were horrified by the idea that their son might be gay, so they went to the leadership of our church, looking for some solution to my 'problem.' Two nights later, I was basically kidnapped from my bed by some church leaders. They took me to a hospital, where they administered an assortment of 'therapies' to fix me."

"Jesus!" he says, his expression pure abject horror.

"So, I don't like hospitals."

"That wasn't a hospital! That was some conversion therapy bullshit."

"Sure. Of course, I know that. But…it was shaped like a hospital, it smelled like a hospital, the so-called doctors wore lab coats and administered treatments as if it were a hospital, but with locks on the doors."

Adam grimaces like my words hurt him. "I'm sorry about before, barging in here and bossing you around. I didn't know—"

"Of course you didn't know. I hadn't told you."

Now he looks up, capturing my gaze with his, and he asks gently, "Are you comfortable with me here, to check your condition as you recover from the concussion?"

I'm surprised he thought to ask, but I'm grateful that he has. It's a gesture of understanding and courtesy, which is greatly appreciated.

Before I can answer his question, there's a loud rumble of racing feet on the stairs outside, and the door bursts open—did I forget to lock that?—to the small redheaded woman I remember as Adam's "date" to the wedding. With a trumpeting shout in a fake British accent, she announces, "Your highnesses, Sir Rufus Woofington of Woofersland, has arrived."

I am so confused right now, but none of that matters when I see Rufus. He comes rushing to me, tail wagging and a big goofy grin across his face. My legs can't hold me when I stand, so I pretty much collapse onto the floor, desperately hugging my dog.

Few things in this world are as pure and special as the love of a dog. His excited whines and wiggles and furious licking have me laughing and hugging him tighter, putting my face in his fur to breathe him in.

All the tension in my body drains out, and the only thing holding me up now is Rufus. He's here, safe and sound, and I can finally relax.

"Speaking of barging in," Adam scowls at the woman, "wow, sister! We're gonna need you to bring the volume level down from an eleven to about a three. He's had a concussion. I can only imagine the havoc your shouting is wreaking on his brain right now."

At this, she looks at me with curiosity, sympathy, and anticipation, as if she's waiting for me to say something. I don't.

Adam speaks instead, gesturing to the woman. "Markus, this is my most annoying sister, Ava."

"Hi, yes, I'm his favorite and bestest sister, and here's your dog, you big cock." *Uh. What?*

Over my head, Adam asks her, "Are you just calling everyone a big cock now?"

"Yes, to avoid confusion."

"I don't think it will have that effect, Sis."

I stare at them as they bicker, and the similarities are so obvious to me now. Their red hair, green eyes, and smirking smiles match almost exactly. I can't believe I didn't see it before. Went so far as to think he was straight and dating a woman who looks eerily like him.

The expression on my face must telegraph my thoughts because Ava turns to me and boisterously explains, "You didn't think we were on a date at the wedding, did you? Ew. No. Siblings." She gestures between them for emphasis, then points at Adam. "Also, by baby bro Rooster here is gay. Like, totally one-hundred-percent homosexual. At the wedding, I wasn't talking about *his* cock, I was calling *him* a cock, because, you know, Rooster. But I don't want there to be any confusion. This cock's cock is, as far as I know, totally available and only stands up for dudes, my dude! So, huzzah!"

Uh. Does my concussion have me hearing things, or did she actually say all that? Because. Wow!

"Ava, for the love of all that is holy, please stop talking and go away," Adam says, with none of the humor in his voice that was there a moment ago when they were bantering.

She stares at him, assessing his expression, then shrugs. "I just want to help."

"Go. Now. Please, Ava."

She turns to me and shrugs again. "Okay, well, I'm gonna go now."

Ava pets Rufus on the head a couple of times, and then she's gone. In her wake, it's very quiet. Rufus and I sit together on the floor. Before us, Adam stands with his hands on his hips, staring at his feet. Quietly, he says to the room, "Well, that was awkward."

"Uh… Huh…" After a few steadying breaths, I return to the conversation we were having before Hurricane Ava made landfall. "As I was saying, I'm a trained medic with over six years in the fire department. I've seen a lot of concussions and just want to ensure you are safe and—"

"Adam, it's all right." Markus's expression softens, and he smiles when he adds, "I trust you."

Well that just blows my mind. He barely knows me, and while a lot of trust comes with the uniform I wear, this feels more personal. It definitely affects me more personally. I grin, feeling truly honored.

With a sigh and a slouch to his posture, he adds, "But I'm exhausted. Do you mind if I lie down for a bit?"

Oh. Shit. Right. Stumbling all over myself, I clear the path between Markus and his bedroom. "Of course. Yes. Rest. Heal. I'll tidy up and make dinner a little later."

Markus nods, stands with slow caution, and shuffles off to the bedroom, Rufus stalwart by his side. The dog presses against Markus's leg like a guide dog steering his human on the right path. What a beautiful sight to behold, this man and his companion, and I watch them until they disappear into the shadowy bedroom and shut the door.

Then I turn around and stare at the kitchen-living room space where I've been left alone, not sure what to do next. In the end, I clean —my go-to stress reducer. My sisters are always trying to convince me to take my stress out on their houses, but in Markus's case, it's a pleasure to turn my nervous habit into something productive for him.

I clean every inch of the apartment, sweeping, scouring, and mopping it all. When that's done, I go down to the clinic to leave a note in the window indicating that, "Due to unforeseen circumstances, we're closed." And while I'm there, I mop those floors too.

When I started, I feared I'd be snooping into Markus's private space, but there is nothing private here. After a couple hours at it, the only personal items I've come across are a few pieces of forwarded mail with a College Station address. No photos, art, notes, or secrets anywhere. The dishes in his kitchen are yellow, and his towels are pale blue, which offers absolutely no insight into the man who rented this place fully furnished. There is a *But First, Pray* script on the kitchen wall, and I'm certain that came with the apartment too. Still, I dust it all the same.

By the evening, I have a stew simmering on the stove. It fills the apartment with the most amazing aroma, and soon enough it calls to Rufus and Markus to follow the siren scent and join me. Markus looks much better; that rest was good for him, putting some color back in his cheeks.

With a warm smile, he looks around at the place, then back at me. "You cleaned?"

"Nervous habit."

"Are you nervous?" He raises a brow with the question.

It's a very sexy look—especially with his sleep-mussed hair—and it does in fact set my nerves atwitter. I try to play it cool. "Idle hands, you know?"

He grins, then looks past me at the pot simmering on the stove. "Smells good."

The subject change is a timely reminder to stop ogling him. Forcing my mind back within the bounds of our medic-patient relationship, I have him sit, then ask to see his stiches. When he nods, I pull up a chair close to him and carefully peel back the tape to take a look. The wound seems to be healing well. No redness or inflammation. I apply a new bandage from my kit, brushing his hair aside so it doesn't get caught in the tape. The strands are so soft, and his skin is so warm...

Stop.

Turning my attention to my medic bag, I focus on packing it back up then stand and set it aside. When I return to the table, I bring the pot of stew, dishing out bowls for both of us. I sit in a different chair, the one across the table from him, safely out of reach.

Markus lifts a spoonful of stew up to blow across the surface before slipping it into his mouth. The expression he makes when he tastes my food is a sight to behold. I wonder if that's anything close to the face he makes when he orgasms, because *damn*.

Stop!

"So your sister seems nice," Markus says.

The mention of my sister takes me completely out of my nefarious thoughts, and I let out an awful noise, an obnoxious cackle. The sound startles Rufus, and I pet him a couple of times to assure him I'm okay. "She's something all right."

Markus nods thoughtfully and takes another bite. Rufus and I both watch but for seemingly different reasons. When he swallows, he asks, "What's the rest of your family like?"

"Loud," I answer with a smile. Markus smiles, too, but he remains silent, like he's waiting for me to continue. And I should. He asked a big, broad question, and I gave him a tiny little answer. Frowning, I swallow the bite of food in my mouth then share some more. "Ava is my youngest sister. There's Alice, Anna, Ava, then me."

"You have three older sisters?"

"Yes."

"That must be—"

"Intense and nightmarish and amazing all at the same time? Yes it is."

Markus chuckles at me, and his smile looks so natural, so easy. Damn, that little nap did a lot for him. He seems so much more comfortable in his own skin now, even as he smirks and casually mentions, "I'm an only child."

"What was that like?"

Markus lifts his eyes to look at me as he considers for a moment, then he finally answers with one word: "Lonely."

I don't know what to say, so I say nothing, watching him as he has another spoonful of his food. As he chews and swallows, his expression changes from something dark to light, like he's preparing to lift the pall that's fallen over our conversation.

"I'll bet you've never been lonely a day in your life," he says with a cheeky smile.

You'd be surprised, is the thought that comes to mind, but I don't speak it aloud. Turning the conversation back to him, I say, "I'm guessing you're feeling less lonely now, too, here in the nosiest small town in America, where the paramedics crash through your front door to render medical care you didn't request."

Markus laughs, and the sound is musical, a whole beautiful song of amusement. When the last chords sound, he pauses, and more somber now, adds, "To be honest, I haven't felt truly lonely in a long time. After my parents had me committed for two weeks, they sent me to boarding school. That's where I met my first boyfriend, and I wasn't lonely anymore."

I grin at the happy ending to such a horrific story, but my curiosity gets the better of me and I need know, "Where's he now?"

Markus chuckles and looks away, running a hand over Rufus. "Last I heard, he went to MIT when I went to A&M."

"The long distance thing didn't work out?"

"No." Now he's fixed his full attention on Rufus, stroking him softly behind the ears. "I was far too focused on school. There was no time for a relationship in my life, especially long distance." Now it's his turn to ask the questions. I know it's coming, but still flinch when he asks, "What about you? Any ex-boyfriends here in Krause?"

I can't help the laugh that comes out. It's a defense mechanism, a way to lighten the subject as I answer, "I've never had a boyfriend."

His brows raise in absolute shock. "But you've… I mean, you've…"

"Fucked? Yeah. I've fucked plenty of men, just no relationships."

"Oh." He blinks and his smile sinks a little. "Why?"

I can think of several good reasons to give him, but they all require long explanations, and that feels like oversharing. Which is absurd considering how much he's shared with me. Still, the only answer I muster is a shrug.

"Hmm," is all he says, but that little sound speaks volumes. He's disappointed in me. We were talking and sharing, and then I stopped. He looks down at his dog again and talks to him now instead of me. "I'll bet you need to go potty."

"Oh. Yeah. It's been a while." I jump to my feet, feeling like a terrible caretaker for not even considering Rufus's needs. "Don't worry. I'll take him for a walk around the block. You can go back to bed, get more rest."

Markus nods, and Rufus and I watch him shuffle back toward the bedroom, the energy from our conversation drained out of him again. I set our empty bowls and glasses in the sink to wash when I return, find Rufus's leash on a hook by the door, and take him out.

Sunset fills the sky with color: deep red, brassy orange, and feathery fuchsia. It's beautiful, peaceful. And down here on the ground, it's peaceful too. The town shops have started decorating for fall with pumpkins on their stoops and faux cobwebs in the windows. I wave at a few of the shop owners, realizing, maybe for the first time, how at home I am in this place.

Small-town Texas is not known for its progressive thinking. In general, it's not an easy life to be gay in a place like this. Yet the people of Krause have fully embraced me. Still, I've never pushed the boundaries of their support.

My father betrayed me when I was ten, and Mom and my sisters chose me over him that day. Later that week, the people of this town chose me too. I know full well the reason for my acceptance here has everything to do with my Mom's deep ties to this community. If I'd been a gay kid in a different family, how different would my life be? I don't know.

Despite this town's acceptance of me, I'm very careful not to strain that good will. And one of the ways I do that is by not dating in Krause. I can't imagine the way tongues would wag if Krause's only gay firefighter were to start dating Krause's only veterinarian. I mean, sure, half the town has been actively trying to matchmake Markus and me, but what about the other half?

Back in the apartment, Rufus goes to the bedroom to join Markus, and I wash the dishes. When that's finished, I sit on the couch, finally letting my exhaustion sink in. After a long, slow shift—punctuated with the nightmare of finding Markus bleeding on that county road— and my nursing duty here, I'm spent.

All I have the energy to do is stare at the wall, and soon I don't even have the energy for that. I lie down. *Just going to rest my eyes*, I tell myself as I pull one of the throw pillows under my head and toe off my boots so I can stretch my legs out. Everything feels heavy. My feet, as I drag them up onto the couch, are like lead weights. With a deep sigh, I stretch and relax.

Just for a moment.

CHAPTER 15

MARKUS

He's gorgeous when he sleeps. Well, he's gorgeous all the time, but when he sleeps, the tension in his face melts away, and all I see is beauty in the arch of his brows, the curl of his lashes, the soft coral color of his lips, the indent of that dimple on his chin…

God, I want to touch him. My fingers itch to reach out and rest my palm on his cheek. I want to wake him and ask him a hundred and one questions about himself. The little he revealed to me over dinner was so enlightening, yet it leaves me wanting.

But he's exhausted. How selfish of me that I didn't even consider he'd come straight from a twenty-four-hour shift to care for me. He stayed up cooking and cleaning when he was probably dead on his feet, if the depth of his sleep right now is any indication.

I pull the blanket off the back of the recliner and place it over him, tugging it down a little so it covers his socked feet. And it's those socks that really get me. They're green with little shamrocks on them. This big, strong firefighter asleep on my couch is wearing St. Paddy's Day socks just before Halloween. God, he's adorable.

Shit. I'm watching him sleep like some sort of creeper. What if he were to wake up right now? How awkward. I step away, and Rufus backs up with me, his nails scraping on the floor.

That's all it takes—that little bit of sound is what wakes Adam. He springs up from deep sleep to wide awake, like someone hit his light switch—off to on in an instant. The sudden movement startles me, and I stumble backward. My knees hit the recliner, and I fall into an awkward sprawl across the chair.

"Oh, Jesus, are you okay?" Adam jumps to his feet, the afghan I just covered him with pooling on the floor. He's instantly in hero mode again, like it's his natural state of being, and sleep is only a slight pause in his programming.

"I...I'm sorry. I didn't mean to wake you."

"Oh." He sort of blinks, then looks back at the couch. "Oh."

He straightens the cushions and picks up the blanket from the floor, folding it and replacing it on the chair like he doesn't want to disturb anything here.

"Is everything okay?" he asks, turning his attention back to me as I stand from the chair. When Adam first arrived here in his work boots, the added lift made it feel like he towered over me. Now, however, with both of us in our socks, we're the same height again. And every part of us lines up so nicely. Our eyes, our hips, our mouths... Breath shudders out of my mouth as I stare at his, and the shape of his full lips, their pale peach hue, the freckle right at the dip of his Cupid's bow.

Crap. He asked a question. What was it? Cute little lines furrow between his eyebrows as he waits for my answer. Finally, I manage to gather my thoughts and say, "Everything is fine. I'm fine, never better. You really don't need to waste another day here. You should get some rest."

What am I saying? Why am I sending him away? I could offer to let him spend the day with me... Sleep in my bed tonight. Would that be weird?

He looks down at his watch, then back at me. He surprises me when he reaches out and places a hand on my cheek. Oh. Is he going to... Are we about to... God, I really want him to kiss me right now.

But he doesn't. Instead he tilts my head up so he can inspect my eyes. After a moment, he seems satisfied by what he sees and slowly nods. "Yeah, okay. I think you're going to be fine, so I'll get out of your hair. Do you need me to take Rufus for another walk before I go?"

Well, shit. I just cockblocked myself. Why am I trying to convince him to leave? This isn't what I wanted. But Jesus, do I even know what I want? Not at all. I like Adam, a lot, but—

Shit, he asked me another question. I don't know what it was, so I just answer, "Sure."

Adam nods and walks over to the leash on the hook by the door. He's taking my dog for another walk? I open my mouth to stop him, to tell him he's already done enough for me, but he's talking so sweetly to Rufus, and Rufus is eating up every bit of the attention.

Behind me, my phone rings on the kitchen table. I shuffle over to grab it, collapse into a chair, and glance at the Caller ID. It's my mother.

Why is she calling again? Her voicemails the last couple of days have just said, "Mark, call me back." Nothing specific, nothing that sounded urgent. And I've been so busy, too busy for an awkward conversation with my parents. But this is the third call in as many days. Something must be wrong.

Still, I hesitate to answer, and my hesitation fills me with shame. I look across the room at Adam, who pretends to ignore me as he snaps the leash to Rufus's collar. Is he wondering why I don't pick up? If this were him, he'd answer his mom on the first ring.

But Adam's family is perfect; they are loving and accepting, while mine is…not. For me, it takes strength to talk to my mother. My hesitation is a defense mechanism. So here I sit, just staring at the ringing thing in my hand while I muster the required energy and armor.

Without a word, Adam and Rufus leave. I listen to their steps as they descend the stairs to the street. At the same time, my phone chimes to indicate a new voicemail. Without listening to it, I call her back.

"It's about time you returned my calls," my mother chides me, without even a hello.

"What's going on?"

She huffs, giving her exasperation a voice. The sound is one I know all too well, a sound that still haunts me from my childhood.

When she finally speaks, I hardly hear her words, and it takes me a moment to process what she's saying: "Your father is dying. You need to come home."

The weather is nice. Still warm, but a cool wind out of the north feels good. Rufus and I walk around the main square in the city center, where he does his business. I use the baggies attached to his leash to clean up, then dump the trash in a city can before we head back. The moment I walk into Markus's apartment, I know something is wrong. Rufus senses it, too, sniffing the air with curious anxiety.

Just then, Markus comes out of his bedroom fully dressed in slacks and a button-up shirt. I stare, a little taken aback with how handsome he looks and a little confused as to why he's dressed at all.

"Good, you're back. I need to leave."

"Where are you going?"

Markus just says, "Mineral Wells."

I frown, and my mind cycles through a whole list of questions. What? Why? When? But the only question that comes out of my mouth is, "How?"

"How?" Markus repeats back to me, clearly confused by my vague question.

I clarify. "Your car was totaled."

"I..." He stammers a little, then just huffs out one forlorn word: "Fuck."

"Why are you going to Mineral Wells?"

He stands with his hands on his hips, staring at the floor like the answer to his problems is there. Finally, he looks up at me. "My dad's sick." I open my mouth to give some sort of response, but Markus has more to say. Not much more, just, "He's dying."

Shit.

A dozen questions come to mind, but clearly, he's in a hurry, so instead of asking them, I offer him the one thing that will help. "I'll drive you."

Sure, I could offer to drive him to a rental car agency, but I don't. Partly because I'm still concerned about his head, and I don't think it's a good idea for him to be driving right now. But mostly because I want to drive him.

He sounds so exhausted when he asks, "Why would you do that?"

His question is valid and one I can't answer yet, not to him and not even to myself. Truth is, I like him. I'm happy when he's around. Our morning jogs have been the bright part of my days these last couple of weeks. So offering to sit in a car with him for the next three to four hours is hardly a hardship.

Tired of waiting for an answer from me, Markus shakes his head. "I can't ask you to do that."

"You're not asking. I'm offering. And besides, with your head injury, I'll feel a lot better knowing you're not driving alone halfway across the state of Texas."

Markus stares at me for a long moment, looking like he wants to argue but doesn't have the energy. Eventually, he just nods. "Can I pay your mom to keep Rufus again? I don't know how long I'll be up there, and he won't be allowed in the hospital, and—"

Is he kidding with this nonsense? "Of course Rufus can stay at Mom's place, and no you're not paying for his boarding. Don't even bring it up. It will insult her." Markus looks truly censured by my statement, and I realize my tone was probably a little too brusque. "I'm just kidding. But seriously, she won't accept payment from you, so don't waste your breath."

"Why?"

"Because, you're my…" Well, isn't that the million-dollar question? What exactly is he to me? A friend? Because I don't generally ogle my friends. More than a friend? I don't even know what "more than friends" feels like. To move us along I say, "You're my friend. Are you packed and ready to go?"

Markus blinks at the rapid subject change, then nods and collects a piece of luggage from his bedroom, wheeling it to the front door. There's no need to take Rufus's leash off, so I crouch and scratch his neck as I let him know he's going to hang with his girlfriend for a day or two.

As I suspected, Mom is delighted to take Rufus in for as long as Markus needs. And when she learns that Markus's father is in hospice, she pulls him in for a long hug.

My mom gives good hugs; it's one of her superpowers. But I've never seen someone so transformed by a hug as Markus is in this moment. He's stiff at first, seeming awkwardly uncomfortable in her embrace. But then he exhales, and it's like he blows all the tension out of his posture with that breath. When they pull apart, Mom clasps her hands on Markus's biceps, saying in the kindest voice, "Rufus always has a place here, and so do you, Markus."

He looks so damn cute, thoroughly confused and maybe even a little overwhelmed by her kindness and open heart. With the smack of a kiss on his cheek, Mom steps past him to me. She squeezes me in those same loving arms as she instructs me to drive carefully.

In the truck, I input our destination into the nav and head north. The drive is easy, just three-and-a-half hours straight up Highway 281 through the central hills and plains of Texas.

Beside me, Markus is on his phone working through his calendar of appointments, explaining to each person he calls that he's had a family emergency and needs to reschedule their visit when he returns. Once he's finally finished, he sets his phone aside with a huff that expresses his deep level of exhaustion.

"All good?" I ask.

"Yes. Finally. But I really need a receptionist."

"Oh yeah? You know, my sister is looking for work right now. Let me know if you'd like to talk to her. She's reliable and smart."

Markus looks at me with an expression of pure horror when he says, "Ava?"

I let out a big belly laugh at his reaction. "No, not that little tornado. She's a cop."

"Ava is a *cop*?"

I chuckle at his astonishment and continue with my original train of thought. "I'm talking about Alice. She and her husband, Clint, had a baby last year, and she quit work to be a full-time mom, but she's losing her mind being home all the time. She's looking for something part-time and flexible that will get her out of the house, and I quote, 'Let her talk about something other than nappies and nipples all the damn time.' "

He chuckles a bit and nods contemplatively. "After, uh, all of this, have her come to the clinic, and we can talk about it."

I nod, making a note to say something to Alice the next time I talk to her. But Markus interrupts my thoughts when he says, "Your family is amazing."

I agree, and Markus doesn't even know the half of it.

Almost speaking to himself now, Markus keeps talking. "I'm surprised my father even wants to see me."

"Illness and death have a way of adjusting priorities."

Markus nods, then, seeming to speak more to himself than me, he muses, "All he ever wanted was a good son… A good, straight lawyer son."

"Instead, he got a gay veterinarian son."

Markus chuckles a bit. "The horror."

He starts to chew on his lip, and I assume that's the end of the conversation. I want to keep him talking, sharing. Maybe I should commiserate? Tell him about the time my father beat the shit out of me when he realized I was gay. My family portrait is only perfect now because he's not in it anymore.

But this car ride isn't about me and my family story. I'm here for Markus, to help him navigate this difficult time. So I stay silent. And I'm glad I do because Markus has more emotions to express.

"Part of me wants to tell you to turn around and drive back to Krause."

I glance over at him, but his gaze is focused out the window. After a moment, I ask, "And the other part of you?"

"Wants to cry because my dad is dying."

CHAPTER 17

MARKUS

At fourteen stories tall, the Baker Hotel is always the first thing you see when you come into Mineral Wells. Once upon a time, it was the first thing you smelled too. The hundred-year-old hotel was built back in the early twentieth century, when people were obsessed with bathing in mineral water. By the sixties and seventies, mineral spas in the middle-of-nowhere Texas had fallen out of favor with the traveling type, and the hotel sat closed and moldering for my entire life in this town.

All I remember about the place is decay. When the wind blew through its many broken windows, across rain-dampened carpets and wallboard, it stunk up this little town with the stench of neglect. Now, though, a company has come in to refurbish and modernize the old place. The spray paint tags have been power washed away, the windows replaced. The old hotel actually looks nice now, and it smells a lot better too.

"Wow," Adam says as he takes in the sight of that sole skyscraper, scratching at the clouds.

And the sky is full of clouds now. From the south, it's been a peaceful sunny day, but ahead of us, the front of a Blue Norther billows and boils with towering shelves of blue-gray clouds. The cold front charges across the plains, promising a violent night of lightning, gusty wind, and torrential rain. I ignore it, all of it. The hotel, the approaching storm—there's already too much on my mind as it is.

Your father is dying. My mother sounded more exasperated than sad when she dropped that bomb. I was stunned silent by the news, so she filled the gap with all the terrible details. My addled mind could only capture bits and pieces. It's cancer, pancreatic. Stage four, metastasized to his liver and lungs. He's chosen to forego chemotherapy. He's in hospice and only has a few days left. He wants to see you.

He wants to see you.

That last part is what keeps coming back to me, those words. My father wants to see me? Why? He's dying. This is what people do when they're dying; they tie up loose ends. Is that what I am? A loose end?

My father and I aren't close. Nothing was ever the same between us after my parents sent me away to "therapy." I stopped sharing my life with them, and they let me. They'd gladly sent me to a boarding school, and I'd gladly gone. When I started college, I left Mineral Wells for good.

I call my parents on Christmas. They call me on my birthday. Yet never, in all the years since I left, have they asked me to come visit.

They're as disappointed in me as a child as I am of them as parents. This town isn't my home, and my parents are just people I used to know. So why would my father want to see me now?

Adam's fist curls over the top of his steering wheel, and he points at the Lone Star Motel as we drive past, saying, "I can drop you at the hospital then come back here and get us a couple of rooms so you have somewhere to rest and decompress... Unless you want me to come into the hospital with you—"

"No!" I answer too quickly, too loudly. That one little syllable is soaked with emotion, and I immediately regret saying it. Taking a deep breath, I modulate my voice. "I really appreciate your kindness in bringing me all the way here, but you don't have to stay. I can rent a car, and—"

"I'm staying the night." Now he's the one who sounds curt, like I've hurt his feelings. But I don't have the energy to consider that or even to apologize and make it right.

At the light, he pulls into the left turn lane and waits for a semi to pass so we can go west to the hospital. On the right side of the road, a group of five crosses stands at the corner where Michael Forest, a star baseball player in the grade above mine, drove his pickup into a minivan carrying the Craine family. Five dead that night. Five crosses now. With the storm brewing ahead of us, it all feels like a portent. It feels like doom.

I look away as we turn, letting my gaze fall on Adam's profile. So handsome, so solid and sure and kind, even to me, someone he barely knows. Clearing my throat, I say, "Thank you for everything you're doing for me. I owe you one…two… Well, I owe you a lot, and I'm grateful."

Adam smirks at me over his shoulder, then pulls into the parking lot and comes to a stop beneath the hospital portico. "You don't owe me anything."

I chuckle. "Well, that's a debate for another day, but yes, I do."

With that, I pop the door open and step out into the harsh wind that pushes ahead of the storm front. Adam and I share a silent nod, and I shut the truck door, turning toward the building. A set of automatic doors detect my movement and slide open for me, and I walk through to the waiting room and the front desk.

I recognize the woman at reception. We went to school together. She probably recognizes me, too, but we don't discuss it. Instead, I ask for my father's room information and then go up to find him.

Stepping off the elevator, Dad's room is across the hall and a window in the door affords me a glimpse inside. There's an array of machines lined against the back wall, their bright displays indicating vital numbers and details, and within that mass of information, is an adjustable bed. There, wired to the myriad machines and tucked beneath the folds of a thick white blanket, is a gaunt old man with sunken eyes and a nasal cannula snaked across his cheeks. His sallow skin looks translucent and waxy, like wet crepe paper draped over a skeleton.

Who is that?

My parents are in their late fifties—by no means old—and in my mind, Dad is still in his early forties. He's the healthy man who jogged every morning, then came in through the back door, huffing and puffing and checking his pulse as I ate breakfast cereal. He's the powerful prosecuting attorney who made criminals tremble with the mere mention of his name. When we last shared a video call, he was looking older and grayer, sure, but nothing like this.

The man in my father's hospital bed isn't him. It can't be.

I stand there, frozen to the spot as I stare into the room, unable to move forward but not able to retreat either. That's when my mother notices me. She's sitting in a chair beside my father's bed, reading a book that she sets down when she comes to the door. The closer she gets, the more she blocks the view of that stranger lying in my dad's sick bed.

My mother looks different too. Older, yes, but there's more to it than just age. She looks weary and tired, and the frown lines etched into her face deepen as she quietly opens Dad's door, then clicks it closed behind her.

"You're here." She sounds surprised, like she didn't expect me to actually show up. To clarify, she adds, "I didn't think you'd make it before he—" She stops talking and leans close, right into my space, which makes me back up a step. Reaching for my head, her tone shifts to accusation as she asks, "What happened to your face? Were you in a fight?"

With everything that's happened today, I nearly forgot about my car accident and the head injury that resulted in twenty-five stitches and a big bandage on my forehead.

I dodge my mother's touch so she doesn't poke at my injury as I answer indignantly. "I was in a car accident. Why would you assume I was in a fight?"

She just shrugs, and I'm left standing there, waiting for her to do something, say something. When she doesn't, I ask, "Can I go in and see Dad?"

"Well, he's finally sleeping. Maybe it's not a good idea to wake him just now."

What? I blink at her, stunned. This morning, she made the situation sound so urgent and dire. I dropped everything to race up here. *Adam* dropped everything to bring me. And now that I'm here, she's literally blocking me from entering his room.

"Where are you staying?" she asks, like we're just having a normal chat.

"The Lone Star up the road."

"Oh, not there. That place is so…unseemly. You could stay at the house—"

"I'm not alone. Is *he* invited to stay at the house too?"

I emphasize the "he" for effect. It's petty, sure, but the longer I stand out in this hallway, blocked from my father's hospital room, the pettier I feel.

"Oh," is all she says. The frown lines worn into her face get some use as she mulls over what to say next to her gay son. "Well… I'll call you when your father wakes—"

"Mom, I've been on the road for almost four hours, hurrying to get here because you said Dad's dying. So I'm going in there now to see him, even if he's asleep."

She stares blankly at me like she doesn't understand what I'm saying. Tired of waiting for her to move, I reach out and clasp my hands on her shoulders, realizing as I do that it's the first time we've touched since I left for college. Gently, I shift her a couple of feet to the right so I can sidestep her to the left and enter Dad's room.

She huffs and mutters something about going to the cafeteria. I ignore her and close the door between us.

Dad's room has only one chair, so I move Mom's book to sit, using a tissue to mark her page. Not wanting to disturb Dad's sleep, I silently watch him as he labors to breathe.

I hate this. I hate that my dad is sick. No, more than sick, he's *dying*. I hate that my dad is dying. And I hate that I don't know if I'm welcome here. Which is absurd—of course I'm welcome here. Mom has been calling me for days to tell me about his condition. Now, here I am, and I have the distinct impression I'm not invited. Did Mom expect me to play the role of a hateful son who ignores his father's dying wish for a deathbed visit?

Well, here I am.

"Mark. You're here." My father's raspy voice startles me.

"Dad." I jerk my eyes up to find him awake, his half-lidded gaze fixed upon me.

"I'm glad you're here. There's so much I want to say to you." His words are wispy, and he takes several pauses to catch his breath as he speaks. He tries to shift positions, wiggling to sit up higher in his bed, but his brittle bones can't do much to move him. I press the button on the adjustable bed so he's elevated a bit more. He nods when it's at the angle he wants, then settles into his new position. All he says is, "I'm sorry."

Uh.

"I'm sorry I wasn't a better father to you."

I'm stunned. His words are clear and coherent, but my brain can't seem to parse and piece them together. "I, uh, what do you mean?"

"I should have supported you, but I let—"

Before he can finish his thoughts, he starts to cough. It begins as something dry and raspy but quickly turns into a violent hacking that seems to wreck him completely, shaking his frail body with bruising force.

Just as I'm about to hit the nurse's call button, Mom comes storming into the room, moving to Dad's side as if she needs to shield him. She mashes on the call button, and when a nurse comes in, the two of them discuss giving him another dose of morphine. When that's done, Dad's cough calms, and his eyes flutter as he finally relaxes in that cloud of blankets. Watching him slip into sleep, all I can think is, "But you let...*what*?"

What was Dad about to say? What was his apology going to be?

I need to hear so many apologies from this man. Was he about to give me one of them? For a moment there, I felt a frisson of hope, something I didn't know I could feel with my parents. But now, it's gone, dormant again as my dad settles into his sleep. My hope withers further when Mom turns on me, her posture aggressive, like I'm the thing she needs to shield Dad from. "What did you do?"

"Nothing."

"You obviously upset him. What did you say to him?"

"Nothing, Mother." I look over at my dad, who's sedated and sleeping now and probably will be for some time. I feel as tired as he looks. And I feel...hungry. Have I eaten today? I can't remember. To Mom, I say, "I'm going to go. I'll be back in the morning."

Then I leave. Mom says something at my back, but I don't hear it. I'm not listening anymore. Exiting the room, I don't wait for the elevator, taking the stairs two at a time to the ground floor.

Outside, thunder rumbles, and fissures of lightning crack open the sky. Rain falls through the fissures and cracks, soaking me to the bone as I walk along the narrow road back to the highway in the direction of the unseemly hotel.

The cold front blows through me, and all around the strobe and percussion of the storm roars and echoes as I rub the rain out of my eyes to look both ways at the highway. It's empty. Everything, everywhere is empty, except for the motel parking lot. There's one vehicle: Adam's truck. I've never felt such relief at the sight of an old Chevy.

I walk across that wide lot so quickly I'm practically running when I reach the door closest to where the truck is parked. The thunder rumbles loudly, so I knock with all my might, desperate to be heard.

It works. He hears me and swings the door open. God, he's breathtaking, wearing nothing but a pair of black boxer briefs. With a glance up and down at me, his eyes fill with worry. Clasping my hand in his firm grip, he pulls me inside and slams the door shut on the storm.

And that's when I kiss him.

Outside, the storm rages. Gusts of wind pelt the plate-glass window with rain, lightning strobes through the crack in the curtains, and thunder seems to shake the whole building. But I hardly notice any of that because I can't stop thinking about Markus.

Lying on my hotel bed with my phone on my chest, I'm ready to slip into jeans and sneakers the instant he calls to tell me he needs a ride. Leaving him at that hospital felt like abandonment. I had to force myself to go through the motions of normalcy, swinging by a drive-through for a burger and fries before checking into two hotel rooms. The food was forgettable, and I can't remember what I've been watching on the television either. All day, my attention has been laser focused in one place, on one person.

The look on Markus's face when I returned from walking Rufus to find him packing still haunts me. The devastation in his eyes from learning his dad is dying, his desperate need to be at his father's side, and the hesitancy to open himself up to the family who hurt him so much—it all squeezes my heart.

I wanted to hug him then. I want to hug him still. I want to comfort and hold him. But he sent me away. So I stay away, waiting, worrying—

A loud bang sounds on the door, not from the wind this time. It's a fist, knocking—an alarming sound to hear coming from a sleazy motel-room door. But instead of being concerned, I feel excited by the sound. Some part of me—the part that's drawn to Markus like a magnet—feels him on the door's other side.

A quick peek through the crack in the curtains confirms it. Markus is standing there, the strands of his dark hair hanging heavy and wet over his eyes, his skin pale and damp from the cold, drenching rain, his posture hunched like the day's circumstances have beaten him down.

My fingers fumble with the security chain and turn the lock so I can swing the door open. From this angle, Markus looks even more forlorn than he did from the window. His eyes seem unfocused, lost, and his posture is weary, like he carries the weight of the whole world on his shoulders. It breaks my heart to see him look so broken. I want to heal him, set him right. Reaching for his hand, I find it shaking from the rain and cold. With a tug, I pull him inside, into the dry warmth of my room, into the calm quiet of this space.

The moment I push the door shut, he lifts his hands to my cheeks. His wet fingers tremble against my skin and chill me with their touch. When he brings his lips to mine, he truly freezes me to the spot.

His kiss is soft. But the instant I have that first taste, I know it won't be enough. I melt into him, my body getting wet as I wrap an arm around his waist and pull him tight to my front. And I melt into the kiss, too, opening my mouth for more, taking his lips now, his tongue. God, he tastes so good, and this feels so right. When was the last time a kiss felt like this? Has any kiss ever felt like this for me, like absolute perfection?

Markus shivers, and I'm not sure if the power of our connection caused it or the fact that he's soaking wet in an air-conditioned room. While I hope it's the former, I assume it's the latter and pull away from his lips just enough to look him in the eyes. His gaze is ravenous. He's as hungry to explore me as I am him. But my inner caregiver is concerned about his shivering and chattering teeth. "You're freezing. Let's get you out of those wet clothes." *Even my inner caregiver wants to get him naked.*

He gives me a cheeky grin and reaches over his head to yank his shirt off, but the top button gets caught on his chin, and he has to wrestle his way out. I would help, but I'm mesmerized. His chest is beautiful, finely hewn muscles that flex and bunch as he works to free himself from the shirt.

I reach out and touch him, tracing my fingertips down the center of his chest until they come to rest on the waistband of his pants. He watches the way I tease at the barrier between us, then his gaze moves up to meet mine, and the heat in those hooded eyes promises so much. He grabs my face again, kissing me hard as I pop the top button on his slacks. Without bothering to unzip them, I shove my hand inside. His cock is rock hard and so hot in my grip, and his groan against my lips is music to my ears.

Grinning with satisfaction at the sounds he makes, I pull away from his kiss and move my mouth to his neck, then make my way south. His skin tastes like rain, and he shivers with each of my kisses, but this time I don't attribute that to the cold. Sliding down onto my knees before him, I work to strip him out of the rest of his wet clothes.

With a careless yank, I unzip his pants, then pull them down along with his boxer briefs. His cock springs up. Finally freed, it stands proud in all its mouth-watering glory. God, that's a gorgeous cock. Markus is beautiful, every inch of him, and I don't hesitate to take him into my mouth, sucking deep until the smooth head hits the back of my throat.

Markus's groan is so damn sexy, and even sexier is how his fingers clutch at my hair. Like he needs something to hold onto, so he holds onto me. But at the same time, he uses his grip on me to direct my movements, telling me with his touch when he needs me to take him deeper, suck him harder. I give him everything he needs, loving the feel of his cock in my mouth, the salty taste of his pre-cum on my tongue.

But I'm not ready for him to come yet. Moving back onto my feet, I take a few steps away from Markus. His hungry eyes follow my every move as I strip out of my boxers. From my bag on the front table, I find the condoms and lube and pull them out. Markus's eyes find mine, and he nods, already agreeing to whatever I want to do next.

I cross the few feet that separate us and don't stop until my body is pressed fully against his. He's breathing so hard, his chest presses to mine with each inhale, and it's a delicious friction. With one hand, I toss the condom and lube on the bed, with the other, I shove Markus backward onto the bed too.

I come down on top of him. We both reach for each other, but this time, he takes over, pushing me onto my back so he can move down my body. When he takes me in his mouth, I holler from the hot heat and groan as his tongue teases the tip of my cock before he sucks me to the back of his throat.

"Oh fuck, Markus, yes. Fuuuck." The words come out like a prayer, and it is. I pray he never stops. With each stroke, he seems to take me deeper, and I am lost to the sensation. My fingers tangle in his hair, and I hold his head still as I top from the bottom, fucking up into his mouth for a few strokes. Not sure how he'll take it, I'm ecstatic when he moans, and the vibration tingles all the way up my spine.

This is too good, and I'm tempted to just lie here and let him have his way with me, but that's never been my style. I push him off me and onto his stomach. Then, rolling on top of him, I crush him under my full weight as I grind my cock against his tight ass and whisper in his ear, "I need to fuck you. Right. Now."

"Yes," he says, and that's all I need to hear.

I pop the lid on the lube and soak him with it as I continue to stroke my cock up and down the seam of his ass.

Once I'm sheathed in a condom and convinced he's ready to get fucked, I coat myself in more lube then press against his entrance. Markus stiffens beneath me but quickly loosens his muscles to let me inside. And with a first solid thrust, I breach his entrance.

"Oh fuck," he gasps.

I give him a moment to adjust, to take me in. But it's only a moment before I push deeper, a shallow stroke that has him writhing and throwing his head back. The tight sinewy muscles of his shoulders and neck flex as his jaw clenches and his hands clutch at the bed.

Slow and steady, I push deeper with each stroke until I'm all the way inside. God, he's so tight. I freeze, gritting my teeth until they hurt, desperate to keep from coming *way* too soon.

When we've both adjusted to the intensity, I really start to move. I'm so desperate, so needy for him, I don't give thought to being sweet or gentle. This is going to be hard and fast, a rough fuck. He bucks up against me, meeting my every stroke with his own. I grab his throat with one hand, forcing his back to arch so I can dominate him with every part of my body, even as I press a kiss against his forehead.

Moving my mouth lower, I kiss and bite his neck until he turns his head to face me, letting me take his mouth with a rough kiss. His hand comes up to the back of my head, his fingers tangling in my hair as he holds me in place, devouring my mouth as I take his body.

This is so fucking hot, *too* fucking hot.

Releasing his throat from my grip, I pull away and grab his hips to bring him up with me when I move onto my knees. Wrapping one arm around his neck again, I reach around with the other and stroke his cock hard and fast, in sync with the rhythm of my hips.

His head falls back on my shoulder, his breaths puffing hot against my ear with each stroke as he takes my cock so well. I want him to take my command, too, so I order, "Come for me. Come all over the bed."

With a gasp and a groan, he does exactly that. His whole body shakes with the force of his orgasm as his cock jerks in my grip and cum streams all over my sheets. Feeling the force of his orgasm as it moves through his body is so erotic and exciting, a powerful sensation that has me coming too. I fuck with the grunting grace of a rutting beast, biting his neck to hold him in place as my orgasm hits so hard I see stars and think I might pass out.

All my strength leaves my body at once, and I go boneless. But Markus is there to hold us both up, hooking an arm around me while I catch my breath and slowly pull out. Then he goes boneless, too, and we fall onto the sheets, making a mess of ourselves.

Markus lets out a lazy sigh as we stare up at the ceiling, and he chuckles a little when he says, "You're really good at that."

Chuckling too, I pull him closer to me. Never one for cuddling, I feel different tonight. I need to be near him, to smell him, and to feel his skin so warm against mine. Like he's a drug, feeding some addiction I didn't know I had. And now I can't get enough.

CHAPTER 19
MARKUS

It takes me a moment to come down from the high of my orgasm. Jesus Christ, Adam is a fucking god. That sex was amazing. We've made a mess, with lube and cum all over his sheets, but he doesn't seem to care and neither do I. Instead, we cuddle, and that feels amazing too. We touch in languid strokes of exploration, his fingers tracing the muscles of my arm as I move my palm over his chest, spreading my cum over him like a claiming. I've coated him in my scent, so he's mine now. It's official.

Except, is it? Is he mine? No. Of course not. I'm getting ahead of myself. This was just sex. It was just sex while my father is consumed by cancer a couple blocks away. I glance around the motel room with its dated orange and navy decor, musty drapes, and lumpy bed. Correction: it was just sex *in a sleazy motel room* while my father is consumed by cancer a couple blocks away.

Christ, what was I thinking? I don't do "just sex." Never have. I'm a relationship guy. But the moment I saw Adam, before we even shared a word, I pounced on him. Did I just use him, coming here to find Adam so I could lose myself with him for a while?

Outside, thunder booms, and the rain keeps pouring. Inside, the flimsy door and single-pane window rattle from the rumble, another reminder of everything I shut out for that brief moment when I was safe and warm and feeling no pain in Adam's arms.

But I'm firmly back to reality now, and I'm starting to wonder something. "When did you pack a bag for our trip? And when did you pack condoms and lube?"

Adam blinks, like I've just yanked him back to reality too. He glances over at the table near the window, where his bag sits open, a pair of jeans hanging out. After a moment, he looks back at me. "I keep a go bag in my truck for…out-of-town trips."

"Trips? Like, for fighting fires?"

"No. I, uh, tend to date outside of Krause."

"Oh." Suddenly, I remember his revelation a day ago: *I've fucked plenty of men, just no relationships.* So this is just another out-of-town *date* for him. "Right."

Now my mind wanders with all the cruel calculations. How many rooms have there been just like this one? How many men just like me? I don't do one-night stands. This isn't who I am. And yet, here I am, another notch on his bedpost, another fuck in his bed.

Sitting up from our cuddle, I look around for my clothes. They're sopping wet and strewn all over the floor, but on the table by the window is my packed bag beside a key to a second room. Extricating myself from his legs and the tangled sheets, I get up and go to my bag, digging for a new pair of briefs and pulling them on.

Adam sits up and frowns at me. When I grab a pair of jeans and tug them on, too, he's quick to his feet, moving so he cuts me off before I leave. "Hey, are you okay?"

I can't hold his gaze; those moody green eyes see too much. So I look down. Which is a mistake as I take in the sight of his cock, still in the condom he wore to fuck me, the condom he had in his go bag, already packed in his truck for just this sort of occasion—a spontaneous hookup in some faraway town.

Grinding my teeth and shaping my lips into a semblance of a smile, I look up. "I'm fine, never better."

I move around him to pick up my wet clothes and stack them

neatly beside my bag, but I can't focus on anything, not with all these thoughts in my head, screaming at me to speak them aloud, questions I desperately need answered.

"Never better?"

Adam startles when I turn quickly to face him. "Why do you date outside of Krause?"

"I…uh…I don't know…" Seeming frustrated, he turns away, and I'm left to stare at the muscles of his back and one very fine ass as he pulls the condom off and walks to the bathroom to toss it. When he comes back, he tugs his discarded boxer briefs on and leans against the wall, crossing his arms over his chest—the chest I smeared with my cum just a few moments ago. His posture is defensive, closed off from me now. "Things are just easier that way."

"What's easier about long-distance dating?"

"It's not 'dating,' it's—"

"Fucking. Right. You said that."

God, I'm so naïve, indulging some fantasy of intimacy with Adam, when he's never indicated that's what he wants. And it's my fault—I'm the one who kissed him. No, "kissed" is an understatement: I pretty much jumped him, without waiting for his consent, let alone a conversation about intentions and expectations.

I kissed him, and he fucked me, and it was incredible, absolutely fucking fantastic, but it wasn't enough. And it's a bit late to start talking about my long-term aspirations now.

Hiding my frustration in a sigh, I pack everything into my bag. "What do I owe you for the rooms?"

"You don't—"

Clenching my jaw so I don't yell, I cut him off to ask again, "What do I owe you for the rooms?"

"Markus, you don't—"

"Look, you did me a huge favor by spending your day driving me here. I'm going to pay you for the gas and meals and the rooms, so what do I owe you?"

He huffs with exasperation—*feeling's mutual*—and beseeches me, "Markus, let's just get some rest. We can sort everything out in the morning."

Yeah. That makes sense. With a curt nod, I reach for the second key on the table and aim for the door.

Adam tries to head me off. "No, I meant—"

"I'll see you in the morning," I say as I swing the door open and leave.

Outside, the storm has moved on, and the rain has eased to a trickle from the eaves and leaves now. There's a new chill in the air; fall finally fell over Texas.

With a bone-deep shiver, I go to the room next door. Sliding the key in the lock, I let myself inside. Only then do I hazard a glance over at Adam's door. He's watching me, looking gorgeous in nothing but his briefs, a deep frown on his lips. I nod my goodnight and then shut the door between us.

CHAPTER 20

ADAM

I can't sleep. Can't get the look in Markus's eyes out of my head, the one I saw when he left me last night. So empty and cut off, like whatever switch had turned him on before was shut down. Lying on that lumpy bed, the smell of sex still rich in the air, I feel weighted with dread, exhausted by…everything.

Up at dawn, I get in a jog before breakfast. The road is wide and flat, so I take the shoulder and run against traffic as I head into town. The historic hotel at the city's center is my halfway point. I loop around it, marveling at the lovely old place that stands tall above everything else here, then go back.

In my room, the shower is practically pointless. Water pressure in this place is pathetic, and the showerhead is shorter than I am, so I crouch and bend and scrub and rinse until I manage to clean myself and change into the jeans and T-shirt from my bag.

That bag is a sour reminder of the conversation I had with Markus last night. He went from being so hot and relaxed in my arms to cold and aloof, rushing to get away from me after I explained about keeping a packed bag in my truck. I try to understand why his mood shifted so abruptly. My sex life is a little bit casual, sure, but he didn't let me explain anything, didn't stay long enough to listen to a word I had to say.

Taking a deep, fortifying breath, I stuff my key in my pocket and knock on Markus's door. He swings it open like he was waiting for me. But nothing in his posture or expression suggests he's glad to see me.

With both of us freshly washed and dressed, it's like all remnants and reminders of our night have been scrubbed away. But, me—I remember.

"Hi," he says with a curt nod.

"Hey."

"I've been thinking"—never a good start to a morning-after conversation—"you should get back home so you don't miss your next shift. I don't know how long I'll be here, and I can't expect you to stay with me the whole time. If you'll just take me by the airport on the other side of town, I can rent a car so you don't have to keep chauffeuring me around."

"Oh." That's all I can think to say. His reasoning is sound and practical, but his passionless tone cuts me to the bone.

It's like last night never happened. I'm used to casual goodbyes after casual sex—it's the script for my entire dating life. I thought this time, though, was different. After sex, we lay together, and I let my mind wander with images of waking up together. Sharing a hot, steamy shower and a morning of soft smiles and stolen kisses. But that was just a fantasy. In reality, all he has for me is indifference as he talks transportation and logistics. No emotion involved.

"Okay. Sure." I'm quick to give him what he needs right now. After all, this is his town and his family tragedy to navigate. If he wants distance from me so he can handle it all, then I'll give it to him. Clearing the emotion from my throat, I add, "Let me pack up and check out, then I'll get you to the rental agency and head home."

Markus nods, but he won't look me in the eyes. He steps back, and the door shuts between us. It feels cold and suffocating, like an avalanche crushing my chest.

Voicing my frustration with a groan, I return to my room, stuff my things into my bag, and toss it into my truck as I head to the hotel lobby to check out. Before leaving, I grab a few granola bars from a vending machine and coffees from the pot steaming beside the front desk—the extent of the continental breakfast offering—then go to my truck and text Markus that I'm ready when he is.

A few moments pass before he comes out with his own bag. He climbs into the passenger seat and silently straps himself in, and everything he does, every movement and breath he takes, seems to hurt me.

This feels like rejection, and I don't get rejected. It's a rule of mine, a rule I've never broken. My relationships are so casual that I hesitate to even call them "relationships," and they are one-hundred-percent rejection free. When I meet someone I like the look of, I make a move. If they aren't interested, I move on. If they are interested, we have a good time, and then I move on. There's no room for rejection in my life, not since that first and worst rejection, not since my dad left. The memories of that awful night flash through my head and send a shiver down my spine.

"I found coffee and granola in the lobby." I gesture to the cup I got for him, and take a sip of my own like it's a demonstration. It burns every inch of my mouth. With a gasp, I caution, "It's hot." Then, changing the subject, I add, "I'd like to redress your wound before I go too."

Adam blinks at me, like I'm not speaking a language he can comprehend. I don't bother explaining anything, just go where the nav tells me to get to the small airport. As I drive, Markus flips the passenger side visor down and pulls the bandage off his forehead, looking at the wound in the mirror, poking at it a few times. When he flops the visor back up and stuffs the soiled bandage into his pocket, I glance over to see for myself how it's healing. All looks well, so I will drop the subject with him, since he seems determined not to speak to me unless absolutely necessary.

The drive southeast of Mineral Wells is flat and empty, not much to see. Marking the entrance to the airport, a T-38 Talon Air Force jet painted in red, white, and blue is mounted on a post, meant to look as if it's flying out of the ground. That's pretty cool, but otherwise, the airport isn't much to speak of. A municipal water tower is the tallest structure around. And two boxy metal buildings that serve as airplane hangars line the narrow runway. The terminal itself is a smaller metal building with a faux stone façade and a row of mailboxes out front.

"There's a car rental desk here?" I ask, very suspicious.

"That's what the map app on my phone says."

"Don't car rental agencies usually have signs advertising their presence, and"—I glance around at the handful of road-weary vehicles parked in the gravel parking lot—"shiny cars for you to rent?"

"The map app says—"

"The app must be wrong. I'll be surprised if that door is even unlocked. Look" —I grab my phone and start searching for the nearest car rental agency —"let's find—"

"It's fine," Markus says as he pushes his door open. "Thank you for the ride."

I reach out like I'm going to grab him, and, what, yank him back into the car? Ten bucks says that wouldn't go over well, so I drop my hand on the center console where Markus's coffee and granola bar sit untouched.

Once Markus has his bag and he's ready to go, he reaches into his pocket, pulls out a wad of cash. and sets it on the seat he's just vacated. It's a stack of hundred-dollar bills, *six* hundred dollar bills. I frown at him. "What's this for?"

"To cover the costs of the rooms, gas, mileage, and, well, everything. This should cover your troubles."

"Six hundred dollars? This whole trip cost one hundred fifty dollars at the most."

"It's for your time too." He smiles. The fucker actually smiles at me as he closes the door.

Oh no he didn't!

I kick my own door open, grab his cash, and storm around the front of my truck to find him at the airport door. He turns back to face me just as I throw the money at him. It rains down to the gravel ground, and he just stares at it as I stomp up into his space.

"Look here!" I yell, and, as if it's an actual command, he looks up and meets my raging gaze as I continue, "I know you're going through something rough, so you can be in a shitty mood, and you can rush off to be rid of me all you want. But I will not tolerate you treating me like your hired escort. Yes, we fucked, and maybe that's uncomfortable for you. But I consider you my friend, and I'd like you to be my friend too. And friends are kind to one another, *for free*, so you can keep your fucking money, Markus!"

When I've said my piece, and I'm huffing and puffing like a raging bull, I give him a moment to give me a piece of his mind, too, but he says nothing. He does nothing except look away, down at his feet and the money scattered all around.

Okay, well, if he's got nothing to say, then this conversation is over. I storm back to my truck, hoist myself inside, and slam the door shut. But I don't leave. I'm one-hundred-percent convinced this is not a car rental agency, and I'm not going to abandon him here in the middle of nowhere, so I drink my coffee and eat my granola bar.

He's lucky I stick around because after he picks up his money and shoves it back into his pocket, he tries the door, and it's locked. I hide a grin behind my coffee cup. It takes him a moment to swallow his pride and walk back over to my truck. I'm sure he expects me to make him grovel, but that's not my style. When he opens the passenger door, I show him my phone screen, where I've mapped out a new route. "There's a car rental agency twenty miles east in Weatherford."

Rather than listen to silence as we drive, I connect the truck to one of my playlists and soon Lil Nas X's "Old Town Road" fills the air, and I sing along with the Billy Ray Cyrus part. Out of the corner of my eye, I see Markus grin, just a little, but his posture eases, and he reaches for his coffee, taking a couple of sips.

Weatherford isn't a big town, but it's twice the size of Mineral Wells, and when we pull up to this car rental agency, the parking lot is paved and filled with shiny, clean rental cars. I feel much more comfortable leaving him here. This time, when he steps out of the truck, he sounds a lot less angry and impatient when he says, "I'd like to at least pay you back for the motel rooms."

With a shake of my head, I say, "Donate it to charity. and we'll call it even."

Markus frowns, but he doesn't argue. I wait again, making sure this door is unlocked, though I know it is. The walls are made of plate glass, and I can see the perky blond behind the counter who grins wide when she sees a handsome man walk into her store.

That's my cue to leave. Cranking my music as I head south toward home, I try to ignore the pain in my chest. Why does it hurt so much? I run through a list of possible medical conditions that might cause this deep gnawing sensation.

Heartburn or heart attack, or could this be heartache? It couldn't be that, could it? I hardly know Markus. But that doesn't seem to matter, because the farther I drive, the more I think about him and the more I fixate on the emptiness of the seat beside me. I miss him. And damn, ain't that a thought.

At a stop sign in one of the little towns this road passes through, I turn on my camera and record a video, talking myself through my thoughts with my followers watching.

"Cock-a-doodle-doo! Hello! Hello! Hello! It's your number one favorite queer fireman Rooster Crows, coming at you live from, well, my pickup truck. Now, as you know, I very rarely stream from a moving vehicle. As a firefighter, I've worked far too many car accident scenes. I take distracted driving very seriously, and you should too. Currently, my phone is in its hands-free holster, so I can focus on the road while I talk through some thoughts.

"And those thoughts are focused on a certain someone. I'm not generally a long-term lover. I'm a casual guy, and I keep my connections casual too. But what does it mean when you want… more? And before you ask, 'What sort of *more* do you want, Rooster?' let me just say, I have no earthly idea. I just, well, I miss someone. And I was just literally beside him thirty minutes ago. I've gone through my checklists, and this ache isn't a heart attack or heartburn, so…that leaves…heartache. Right? I guess I'm looking for some expert opinions here. Help me understand: How do you know when you like someone, like, really like them…as more than just a friend?

"Jesus, I sound like a teenager gossiping in the school cafeteria. Okay, enough of this nonsense. If you have thoughts, leave them in the comments, and I'll check them out when I'm not driving. Ciao, my brood."

Immediately after I stop the recording, I regret even making the video. Sure, I share a lot about myself online, but never anything as personal as talking about a guy I'm into. Probably, because I've never been into a guy like this. Still, I need to delete this video. When I get home, I will.

But I don't go home. When I reach town, I go to Mom's house instead. Because there is really only one cure for the sour mood I'm in: puppy therapy.

Mom and Alice are in the kitchen, cooking something that smells amazing, and my niece Avery is in her high chair, kicking her little feet and giggling at me. I give Mom and my sister hugs then make funny faces at my niece before I exit out the back door and cross the yard to the kennels.

Drusilla and Rufus are excited to see me, their tails wagging their whole bodies as I let them out of their adjoining pens. The purity of their affection fills my heart. I trade head scratches and back rubs for sloppy kisses and tail wags, and it is rejuvenating.

Grabbing a tennis ball out of the toy bin, I have them fetch a few. Drusilla can't keep up with Rufus, so she resorts to ambushing him as he returns the ball to me.

"Everything okay?" Mom asks from behind me, and I startle.

She loops an arm around my waist, and I rest my arm on her shoulders. Together we watch the dogs as they wrestle and roughhouse, the ball forgotten.

"It is now," I answer with a smile.

"Why don't you stay for dinner? We're making a roast. And you can spend the night. I'm sure these two lumps would love to share your old bed with you."

I chuckle at the idea of spending a night in my childhood bedroom with the dogs. Before answering, I check my phone for any missed calls from Markus. I've been checking every few minutes since I left Mineral Wells. Nothing.

"Sure, Mom. Sounds good."

Mom hugs me a little tighter, seeming to sense I need it. She could always tell when I needed the comfort and support of my family. She doesn't push for me to explain, and I'm grateful. Instead, we just stand together, watching the dogs play in the waning light of the setting sun.

CHAPTER 21
MARKUS

Adam's scent is everywhere. Even after two showers, he's all over me. His taste lingers, too, resistant to toothpaste and mouthwash. He left me an hour ago—dropped me off at a car rental desk one town over, then drove away—yet he lingers in my head.

I groan audibly, and a nurse glances at me, looking concerned. Giving her a quick grin, I wait for her to walk past me, then duck my chin and resume staring at the floor in front of Dad's room.

God, I really don't want to go in there. I'd rather be in Adam's truck right now, the heat blasting from the vents in the dash as he butchers every song he sings along with his playlist. I shake off those thoughts—and the little grin they give me—as I look through the rectangle of glass in Dad's door, offering me a glimpse inside the room.

Aside from the passing nurse, no one has noticed me lurking out here yet. What am I waiting for, a written invitation? Step forward once, twice, and go inside. Simple. Except… Should I knock first? Probably. If I were to visit my parents' home, I would knock on the door. I should knock here too. So I knock.

Mom looks over, and she must be expecting someone else because her smile sinks when she sees me. Quickly, she pastes it back on and comes to let me in. When she has the door open, she glances over my shoulder, as if checking to see if I've brought the man I alluded to last night.

When she determines I'm alone, she silently moves aside so I may enter. Every step I take into the room stirs the air around me, and I smell Adam again, like his spirit clings to my skin and movement stirs him awake. I wonder if my mother can smell his musky scent on me too. If she can, she doesn't let on. She's pretty much ignoring me, as usual.

"Mark." My father's scratchy voice, and his use of my old name, jolts me out of my thoughts and right back to reality. He's exactly where I left him last night, completely unmoved, but he looks sicker, weaker, his color is a jaundice yellow today.

"Dad," I say with a nod as I move toward him. "How are you feeling?"

Jesus, what a dumb question. He's dying, *you asshole.*

My father opens his mouth like he intends to answer, but before he can, my mother speaks for him. She flutters around like a hummingbird, straightening his blankets and adjusting his pillow as she explains that he's feeling restless and can't sleep, how his feet and hands are swollen from water retention, and he's suffering from abdominal pain.

After more than a minute of Mom's constant chatter, my dad tries to speak, but the effort causes a coughing fit, which has him wincing in pain as he struggles for breath. The weakness I see in my father has a profound and devastating effect on me. As far back as I can remember, my father was larger than life. His disapproving specter loomed over every decision I made, either inspiring me to cave to his wishes or rebel in defiance. Either way, his shadow was always there. And now, seeing that big man reduced to such frailty throws my world off its axis.

Rushing to help him, I go to one side of his bed while Mom goes to the other. Each of us tries to tend to his needs, and it's like a competition I didn't realize I'd entered. But now that I'm here, I fight to win. I find a cup of water on my side table and reach for it, holding it for Dad so he can take a few shallow sips.

When his coughing fit subsides, he groans in pain and holds his abdomen. Clearly concerned, Mom starts up again with her fluttering, but this time she tries to order me around like an employee. "Mark, go ask one of the nurses if there is anything they can give him for this cough. It's causing him such discomfort, and—"

"Candice, why don't you go find one of the nurses yourself." Dad suddenly finds his voice, and the harshness of his tone freezes us both. "I need to talk to Mark…and I can't when you keep yapping."

Uh.

I glance between them, astonished to see any sort of rift there. In all my youth, they never argued. Sure, they argued *with me*, but never with each other. They were a united front in the fight against their unruly, ungrateful, unholy son.

My mother stares at him for a moment, seeming as stunned by his irritable outburst as I am, then she mutters, "Very well," and leaves the room.

When she's gone, and it's just the two of us, I'm crushed by another of those avalanches of guilt, like their tiff is somehow my fault. But then, I've been accepting blame for their issues all my life. I'm done with that.

Instead, I loosen my shoulders, like that will unburden me somehow, and make my way to the chair beside Dad's bed. When I'm settled, I turn my attention to my father, ready to listen to whatever it is he feels he needs to say to me.

"I should apologize to her," Dad says. His voice sounds scratchy, and his words come stilted, spoken after each puff of oxygen delivered through his nasal cannula.

"I guess," is all I can manage to say.

"I owe you an apology too." He surprises me with that revelation, and I startle when he tries to grasp my hand.

It takes me a moment to realize this is him reaching out, literally and figuratively. I can't remember the last time my father touched me. Even when he thought I was the son he wanted, he rarely hugged me. Once he learned my truth, he never hugged me again.

But now, he reaches for me, and I accept his hand in mine. He's fucking dying, after all. If I don't give him this one small kindness, I know I'll regret it. His grip is frail, like he's made of glass, absolutely breakable. So I try not to squeeze too hard, stroking my thumb over his crepe-paper skin, which looks almost purple from the veins that spider around his bony knuckles and down his fingers.

"Mark, er, Markus, I'm sorry…"

To hear his voice again after such a long pause is jolting, but the words he says are what really surprise me. He called me Markus. *Finally*, he called me by my chosen name. And… He's sorry? For what? Which part? I need more, need to understand exactly what he's sorry for, but he's already winded from saying so little. So I stay silent, watching his bloodshot eyes as he stares back at me, catching his breath to speak again.

"I should have…tried harder…to know you." He runs out of air as he speaks, and the words sound like ghosts of themselves. He takes a few moments to breathe in more of the oxygen, then continues. "Your mother…wanted to *fix* you… And I let her."

Yes, I remember. I'll never forget. Between praying for me and wailing with shame, she'd tell me, "Paster Samuelson can fix this. He can get you back on the path of righteousness."

"But," Dad gives my hand a weak squeeze and breathlessly finishes, "you were never broken."

I can't believe what I'm hearing. With his voice so weak, I wonder if I'm actually imagining this, hearing what I want to hear in his whispered words. Could it be a side effect of the concussion I suffered a few days ago? Or, maybe it's his illness that is causing this miscommunication. Is aphasia a symptom of pancreatic cancer? Is he trying to tell me something else, but the wrong words keep coming out of his mouth?

One glance up at my father's face tells me everything I need to know: he means what he's saying. His eyes shine with tears, and one falls down his cheek. The sight of it—this once proud man who *never* cried, shedding tears because of me—hits me with a tidal wave of emotion. It's more than I can handle, more than I can even comprehend.

With his voice weak and watery, he adds, "Markus, I failed you, in so many ways, and I'm sorry."

My vision blurs with tears, and I wipe them away with my free hand. With the other hand, I squeeze his, not too hard, just enough to let him know I'm still holding on. But tears clog my throat, and I can't speak. It feels pathetic. My father is dying, yet he managed to speak his mind. Now, when it comes to me, I'm mute.

That's when my mother returns. She has a nurse in tow, but Mom is the one doing all the talking. She's like the stage manager to Dad's death, telling people where to stand and what to do. She expects me to stand up from the chair I occupy, but I'm not willing to let go of Dad's hand for anything. This is the only connection I've had with him in years.

The nurse senses the standoff and hustles out the door, quickly returning with a second chair. Mom huffs, a sound that is equal parts appreciation for the chair and frustration with me. While the nurse is here, she explains to Dad that they can give him a cough suppressant and another boost of the pain medication, but it will make him drowsy. Dad looks to me, as if wanting me to decide. I nod. He's clearly in pain. As nice as this conversation has been, I do not want him to hurt.

The nurse injects the medications into Dad's IV drip and tells us she'll check in with us in an hour or so. I ignore her and everything else happening around us, just focusing on Dad's bloodshot gaze as his eyelids grow heavy with drowsiness, and finally I manage to say the words I think he needs to hear.

"I forgive you, Dad, and I'm okay."

"But seriously, why would you bring teeth to a cuddle puddle, Princess Drusilla? Put those chompers away, little girl." I admonish the puppy, who looks thoroughly ashamed of her bad behavior.

Sweetly, she licks my wrist where she just nibbled on me. I give her a pet and whisper endearments as she turns to kiss my cheek and ear. When I try again to arrange the blanket over me. Drusilla spots my toes twitch under the fabric and attacks. This time, thankfully, Rufus comes to my rescue. The big boy rolls his formidable weight onto her, pinning her and giving her a new target for her playful energy.

There's not a lot of room in my childhood bed, definitely not enough room for a full-grown man and two large dogs, but we're making it work, and the silliness of the situation is enough to distract me from, well, everything else. But when my phone rings, "everything else" is suddenly top of mind again.

Markus is *finally* calling me. But why now? It's after midnight. Is something wrong? I scramble to answer and clear my throat so I can manage to sound casual. "Hey."

"Hey," Markus says back. His voice is both a jolt of electricity that zaps through me and a balm that soothes my soul. I sit up on the bed, and that attracts the dogs' attention. They watch me closely, their intense gazes seeking to detect the nuances of my mood.

After a moment's hesitation, Markus starts again. "I wasn't sure if I should call. It's late, and I know you work tomorrow."

"Next shift starts tomorrow at noon." My response sounds curt, like I'm mad at him. I'm not. I got over my anger during my drive home from Mineral Wells. Now, it's a blend of confusion, exhaustion, and a pinch of loneliness that make up this mood I'm in.

"Oh. Well, I hope I'm not disturbing your sleep, or—"

"You're not." I'm quick to interrupt any notion he might have to hang up. I want to talk to him. But when he doesn't say anything more, I jump in. "I'm glad you called. How are you? How is your father?"

Markus takes a deep breath and lets it out as a heavy sigh, then says, "I'm okay. And my father is…well, dying."

"Right, dumb question." I grimace at my stupidity for bringing up the subject. Markus's story of his parents' refusal to let him be himself has colored them in a negative light for me. But they're still his parents, and I know he's hurting with all of this. "I'm sorry."

"No." He says the word almost like he's yelling it, but in a hushed tone, like he's yelling it in a library, or, well, a hospital. "*I'm* sorry. I'm so sorry."

That shuts me up. Lying back down, I pet the dogs as I stare at the ceiling, the unmoving blades of my fan casting long shadows from the glow of the nightlight my mom keeps in here. I leave a long, silent gap for Markus to speak.

So he does. "I was an asshole to you, and I'm sorry. You went out of your way to help me. I mean seriously, you went *two hundred miles* out of your way! You did me all these massive favors, and I was a complete dick to you."

I've never been good at receiving compliments or apologies, always turning them into a joke. And, apparently, I haven't cured myself of that tendency. "*Massive favors*? Is that what the kids are calling it these days?"

"Uh. I… meant…"

Markus's tongue-tied stammering is adorable, but I quickly put him out of his misery. "Sorry, dumb joke. I'm glad I could help—"

"I like you." Markus's words come on a gust of breath, like he's forced them out of his throat.

Uh.

"I like you a lot, and I don't know what that means to me, or to you, but I wanted to find out, and then I got the call about my father, and, well, I pretty much tackled you when we…you know…and now my emotions are a mess, and I wish I hadn't been such a jerk to you this morning because even if you don't want anything more from me, sexually speaking, I would still like to be your friend."

Jesus, that was *a lot* of words, a lot of words I didn't realize I wanted to hear from him. I sit up, and the dogs grumble at the position change. My mouth flounders open and closed as I consider what to say in response. I like him, too, of course I do, but—

"Wait. Uh… Shit. Something's wrong. I have to go."

And with that, he hangs up on me.

My dad is dying. Not in that casual "he's in hospice, and only has a few days left" type of dying. He's actively dying right now.

There I was, out in the hallway, stealing a moment alone to call Adam, when chaos erupted in the form of my mother, standing outside Dad's door hollering for help.

Now, a couple nurses enter Dad's room. Mom's voice peaks in volume, the sound hurried and worried and in great contrast to the staff's calm, clinical demeanor.

Hesitating just a moment, I step into Dad's room and freeze at the foot of his bed, watching the staff work as my mother begins to pray through her tears. I don't have tears to shed or prayers to add, unless you count my hope for a peaceful and painless passing.

With do-not-resuscitate orders in place, no one tries to restart my father's heart or force air in and out of his lungs. We all just stand there and let him die.

Once he's passed, a new ritual begins. The post-death procedures start with turning off the equipment surrounding the bed, silencing the mechanical tones and beeps until it is deathly quiet in here. Wordlessly, the staff files out of the room so we, the family, can have a private moment alone with our dearly departed.

But I don't need a moment alone with my father. My last words to him were of peace and forgiveness, and I'm glad for that. Coming here, sitting with him as he slept today, allowed me some closure on a relationship that was never what I needed, but at least at the end I wasn't left with an empty hole and no farewells. Do I have unanswered questions? Yes, of course, but they feel less important to me now.

My mom, on the other hand, seems to need this moment. She cries, her tears dripping and dribbling down her cheeks as she holds her husband's limp hand.

Suddenly, I feel a wave of sorrow for her. I spent today mourning my father as he lay dying, but he's gone, and now is when the pain truly begins for those left behind. Mom is a widow now, and she's completely alone. Wanting to comfort her, I set my hand on her shoulder. She jerks with shock, and glances up at me as if she didn't realize I was still here.

"I'm sorry," I say to her, and the words have layers of meaning: sorry for startling you; sorry for your loss; sorry we are the way we are to each other.

Her reaction is to turn her attention to her appearance, dabbing a tissue on her cheeks to dry her eyes and the tracks of her tears, like she's been caught doing something she shouldn't be doing. As if revealing emotion is a terrible sin. When she stands and turns to face me, the emotional creature I caught crying is gone, and in her place is a planner, making plans.

This is the mother I've known all my life. Emotion was never her style. She starts talking, and there's no sign of tears or sorrow in the tone of her voice as she rattles off the particulars of her plans for Dad's final arrangements.

In overly specific detail, she tells me that the hospital will send Dad's body to the funeral home, and in four days, there will be a service at their church, then the burial in a double plot they purchased a couple years ago at the big cemetery on the edge of town.

"Mark..." Mom starts.

I know with frustrated certainty, that no matter how many times I tell her I go by Markus now, she will only ever call me Mark.

"You'll need to call your father's former law partners to give them the news." Mom is reading from a list now, something I suspect she's been making for the last couple days.

"Mother," I interrupt her before she gets too far into her assignments for me. "I'm not staying for the funeral."

"What?" She frowns, pales, looks truly aghast. Then her horror turns to anger, and she scowls at me. "That's it? You're just *leaving*?"

"Why would you want me to stay?"

"To honor your father, to show respect for your family. How will it look if our only son misses his own father's funeral?"

"I'm not concerned with how it will look. I said goodbye to Dad in the way I needed to. Thank you for calling so I had that opportunity. The funeral is for you and your community. I'm not part of that." I move toward the door, ready to leave.

"You've always been so selfish, such a disappointment." Mom's words hiss, like she's a snake trying to bite.

I don't let her get to me. Mom's contemptuous distain has bitten into me for decades, and it's always hurt. She's taken parts of my peace, happiness, and identity, but today I won't let her hurt me anymore.

"Goodbye, Mother," I say, and then I go.

The chill in the pre-dawn air ushered in by last night's cold front is cool and crisp and smells like chimney smoke. It's one of my favorite scents, and fall is my favorite time of year, so I drive with the windows down. I'm not dressed for the cold, but it feels invigorating as it whips and swirls through the car.

Each mile I drive away from my hometown feels good too. I have no idea how much it will cost me to return this car in a different city from the place where I rented it, but I don't care. I just want to leave, as quickly as possible, rental car costs be damned.

The drive home to Krause feels like an exorcism, a cleansing of so much negative energy, surfacing deep, dark emotions that have festered inside me for far too long. When the sun crests the horizon, harkening the start of a new day, it burns away some of my old pain. My vision blurs and I try to blink away the tears, but eventually I need to pull over as emotion overtakes me. I let it, sobbing fiercely, like a howling animal.

Apparently, my exhaustion caught up with me, because I wake on the side of that road when a semitruck blasts past me, shaking the ground and the shoulder of the road and my rental car parked atop it. The truck's wake blasts an icy wind through my windows, twisting and tangling my hair as it slaps and prickles my chilled skin.

I'm awake! Yep.

Rubbing dry bits of tears and sleep from my eyes, I stretch my aching muscles. When I'm truly awake again, I restart the car and continue. Soon, I'm back in Krause, and my spiritual journey home is at an end.

Checking the time, I see it's just after noon. Adam's on duty at the fire station now. I wanted to talk to him before he started his shift because I hate how I left things between us last night, declaring my "like" for him and then hanging up. But I will have to wait for my opportunity to sort that out.

In the meantime, I have shit to do.

First stop, Krause County Sheriff's Department. The county's law enforcement unit is housed in a small brick building a couple blocks from my clinic, large enough to fit a two-cell jail and the workplace of Sheriff Sneed and four deputies. Considering it's the middle of the day, I expect to walk into a bustling office, but it's deserted, all the desks empty.

I stand around, feeling like an idiot who doesn't know the protocol here. Is there a bell or something to ring for service? Looking all over, I find nothing like that, so I finally resort to hollering, "Hello?"

"Hello?" I hear back, almost like an echo, except the response comes in a feminine voice.

Despite this call and response, no one appears in the front office to greet me, so after a few moments, I try again, putting a little more singsong into my tone. "Hello?"

"Hello?" she replies, putting more singsong into her tone too.

What the actual fuck?

"I've come to check on my car. I was involved in an accident a few days ago, and I was wondering where it was towed—"

"Oh, hey, Markus!" The voice says again, but this time it's accompanied with the face to go with it as a woman comes out of a doorway along the back wall. She's tiny and looks a little overwhelmed by the heavy belt and it's law-enforcement accoutrements weighing on her trim hips. Her red hair is pulled back into a tight chignon, which makes her big green eyes seem even larger as she smiles up at me.

Wait, how does she know my name—?

"Don't tell me you've forgotten me already," she says and winks at me, like she can read my mind.

Truth is, I have, but I try to play it cool. I fail, just muttering, "Uh," stupidly.

"I'll give you a hint," She leans on a chair and with a dramatic slur to her speech says, "Dance with me, you big cock."

Oh. My. God. It's Adam's sister. And instantly I remember he'd mentioned she was a cop. Wow. I should have recognized her by the red hair and green eyes, but she looks very different in a uniform. "Ava! Of course, how could I forget you?"

"That's Deputy Newman to you, when I'm on duty," she says with a cheeky grin and lifts two fingers to her forehead in a salute. Then she cracks up laughing at herself. My god, she's so strange and adorable, and her smile reminds me of Adam. I smile too.

"Okay, so, car accident, car accident," she mutters as she spins on her heels and walks away from me. Her lithe steps make it look like the heavy utility belt weighs nothing at all. She goes to one of the cabinets against the wall and riffles through it, then shouts, "Aha!" as she pulls out a file and crosses to a copy machine.

Once she's returned the original file to its cabinet, she brings the copies to me and starts shuffling through the pages as she speaks. "Now, what you're gonna do is take this sheet to the garage, your car is at Howard Teddy's place over on Pecan Street. Tell Howie you want to see your vehicle and take pictures for your insurance claim. He's gonna try to talk you into a front end repair, but between you and me, that car was totaled, chassis bent all to hell. It's salvage, so just clear out your belongings, file your claim, and get yourself a shiny new car."

"New town, new car, new me?" I say, trying to match her chipper tone with my own.

"Exactly! I knew you were a smart one!" She pokes me in the belly like I'm the Pillsbury Dough Boy. Jesus, she's intense.

"Okay, well, thank you for the info." I angle toward the door, ready to leave before she overloads me with more information or pinches my cheek or something. But, before I go, I ask, "How's Mildred?"

"She's so hardheaded, hardly felt a thing. That girl is already back to work at the library. Doctors are looking into what might have caused her to lose control and veer into your lane, though. Think she might of blacked out, but why she blacked out is the question now."

Adam was right about the gossip in this town. It's unlike anything I've ever experienced.

With an awkward little wave, I open the door to leave. "Well, I'm glad to hear she's okay. Ready to get back to work at the clinic too. It was good seeing you."

"Good seeing you too. And I better not catch you getting up to any trouble," she says in her deputy sheriff tone.

Outside, I get back in my rental car. Next stop: Adam and Ava's mom's place to pick up Rufus. Then we can grab some groceries and settle in for a cozy evening, a hearty meal, and a good night's sleep before reopening the clinic tomorrow.

Sounds like heaven to me.

This is heaven, indeed. But truly, is there anything more heaven sent than the unconditional love of a dog? Rufus excitedly whines and huffs as he wiggles his whole body.

"Nothing quite like the purity of a dog's heart. Like chicken soup for the soul, ain't it?" Adam's mom, Angie, says as we walk across her backyard to the kennel shelter.

The moment Angie opens the door to Rufus's corral, he comes at me. All ninety pounds of muscle hit my legs so hard he knocks me back a few steps. Recovering, I come down onto my haunches so I can get close to him and wrap my arms around his neck. He calms with my nearness, letting out a long sigh as I press my nose to his head and breathe in his doggy scent.

To Angie, I agree, "Indeed, it is. Just what the doctor ordered." To Rufus, I whisper, "I missed you, too, big guy."

At the sound of my words, he licks me. First, slowly, almost timid, but soon he's got his tongue working overtime as he licks my ear and neck and chin. When I pull away a little to laugh at him, he aims that thing at my mouth, and I laugh as I hold him back. He turns his attention to my cheeks, fixated on licking them clean. Only then do I realize I'm crying, and he's licking my tears away.

"Rufus had a good time last night at his slumber party with Rooster and Drusilla, but clearly this boy missed his daddy." Angie watches our reunion with a sweet smile, kindly not commenting on my tears as I wipe my face dry and push to stand.

Also, what did she just say? Adam spent the night with the dogs? After I'd been such an ass to him, he came back here and took care of my dog. Clearing my throat, I say, "I missed him too," and that *him* could apply to man and animal, both.

A woman bouncing a chubby little cherubic baby on her hip joins us. She—and her child—look just like the rest of Adam's family. It seems that Adam is the only tall one in the bunch, but aside from that disparity, they all sport the same red hair and green eyes, which unmistakably identify them as Newmans.

"Hey, boss!" she says, and at first, I think she's talking to Adam's mom, calling Angie "boss" for some reason.

When both women stare at me expectantly, I point at myself, asking, "Are you talking to me?"

She laughs at me and her baby tries to stick his fingers in her mouth. "Yes! Rooster, mentioned you were hiring a front office assistant, and, well... I accept the job!"

Oh. Okay. I chuckle at her, but don't argue. "You must be Alice. Great to have you on board. When do you start?"

"Tomorrow. Also, I hope you won't mind if I bring this little milk fiend with me most days. Grandma can only babysit so many times before she starts complaining that she has her own life to live." Alice says that last part in a voice that I can only guess is a poor impersonation of her mother.

My theory is confirmed when Angie rolls her eyes at her daughter. Kissing her grandchild on the cheek, she starts walking toward the house, hollering back, "I'll leave you two to talk business. Markus, you're welcome to stay for dinner."

I smile wide at the family interaction, in complete awe. And without even thinking about it, the words fall out of my mouth. "Your family is perfect."

Alice furrows her brow, like she's not following my train of thought, but she reluctantly agrees. "We have our moments."

"Trust me—you're perfect."

Alice chews on her lip for a moment and holds her baby a little tighter before she speaks again. "Has Rooster ever told you about our dad?"

I shake my head.

"Ask him sometime."

"What if I ask you?"

She wags her finger at me like I'm a bad boy for asking. "That's not my story to tell. But I think you need to know. Cuz I think"—she angles her head to give me a thorough once-over—"you're someone who needs to know everything about Rooster."

What a cryptic thing to say. I'm intrigued.

"But in the meantime, you should check out his YouTube channel."

Wait. What? "Adam has a YouTube channel?"

Alice nods so big the gesture makes the baby giggle. "Yes! It's great! He's started posting on TikTok, too, if that's more your thing. But he's had his Rooster Crows channel on YouTube for ages."

Rooster Crows? Adam has a TikTok account *and* a YouTube channel? Now that is *very* intriguing. Any notion of staying for dinner is out the window. Clearly, I need to get Rufus home so we can relax and watch some YouTube videos.

Rooster Crows appears to be an extreme version of Adam. His friendly, casual nature is there, but it's turned up to eleven. He has the same cheeky humor but with a brashness added in for the audience. He uses a different voice too. It's more chipper, like the voice he uses when he speaks to the dogs.

The videos he posts seem extremely personal but guarded at the same time. For instance, while he speaks openly about his life as a gay firefighter in small-town Texas, he's careful not to share the name of our town.

I started watching a video that is ranked as his most popular, a workout video he posted a little over a year ago. He's talking us through his warmup for leg-day exercises, and the yoga poses he does to work his glutes are... Christ, it's no wonder this has millions of views. I want to play it on repeat as I fall asleep each night, a workout lullaby guaranteed to bring pleasant dreams.

Next, I watch a video of Drew and Chloe's wedding. It's a sweet tribute to them, with some gorgeous footage of the happy couple interspersed with amusing moments of wedding hijinks, and then right at the end there's me. I look bewildered as Dee drags me around by the elbow, and I can hear Adam chuckle when she brings me to stand right before him.

Clearly, I'm mesmerized by the man holding the camera, completely enchanted. Everyone in the comments section sees it, too. They all want to know more about the hot, moon-eyed man, speculating on who I am and what I mean to Adam. He hasn't replied to any of those comments, keeping my identity secret. His protection is appreciated, but I sort of wish I knew what he thought of the moon-eyed man as well.

There's a new video. It's just a day old, and the thumbnail suggests Adam took it while in his truck. I go to click on that one but pause when I hear a noise downstairs. Rufus hears it, too, a sudden rattling, and his whole body goes into high alert, his ears perked up to listen.

My heart races at a gallop as I consider the possibilities. Could it be the wind? Is it windy tonight? Probably just a family of racoons who've found their way into the diner's dumpster in the alley behind my building. Or could it be opossums? The opossum is one of my favorite animals, and the only marsupial native to North America.

A crash comes from downstairs, and I can no longer fool myself into thinking it's a goddamn marsupial riffling through garbage. Someone is breaking into my clinic.

Rufus stands at attention and lets out a very loud, very aggressive bark. I gesture for him to be quiet. He's issued his warning to the intruder, and now I can listen, to determine if that bark did the trick.

But what I hear is the crack and crunch of glass underfoot as someone steps into the front office, then hurried footsteps on the clinic linoleum as they move through my space. My fear is immediately replaced by blind, stupid rage.

Seriously, Universe? Why? You cracked my head open as you wrecked my car, then dragged me to hell to watch my father die. Wasn't that enough for you?

Springing to my feet, I run to the back set of stairs in the kitchen. I should bolt the door, call the police, but anger clouds my judgment. And the surge of adrenaline pumping through my veins inhibits my ability to make rational decisions.

Swinging the door open, I race down the stairs. Rufus is in lockstep beside me. We're not quiet about it. Anyone downstairs would surely hear us coming. So I'm surprised when I open the door at the bottom of the stairs and spot a man only a few feet away. His back is to us, hunched over as he leans his weight onto a crowbar, trying to break into my narcotics safe.

"Stop what you're doing, and leave." I'm proud of the tone of my voice, so much authority and very little tremble in my words.

The man jumps as if he truly hadn't heard us coming. He spins awkwardly and squints like the light coming from the stairwell behind me is as blinding as the sun.

"You're not supposed to be here," he says with a voice that cracks like he's parched, dying of thirst. He looks starved, too, but it's not food he craves. Pretty sure he's after the ketamine I keep locked in that cabinet.

I don't like how twitchy the guy is, his eyes darting around the room and his pupils blown wide like he's high on meth. And I really don't like how his fist keeps flexing as he clutches that crowbar in his grip, as if it's transformed from a tool to a weapon in the last few moments. So I warn again, "Leave. Now. And nothing will happen to you."

The man doesn't make a move to go. Instead, he turns his gaze to Rufus, eyeing him like he's calculating the odds of besting my dog. The odds are zero percent, buddy. When he squeezes his grip on the crowbar again, I consider the movement a threat. Apparently, so does

Rufus. He growls deep and low, a terrifying rumble that should scare sense into anyone.

Not this man. Lifting the crowbar like he wants to swing it at my head, he takes a step toward me. That's as far as he gets before Rufus's protection training kicks in, and he attacks.

Charging with all his strength and weight, Rufus pushes the man off-balance. It doesn't take much, and the wiry guy teeters backward, his crowbar clattering to the ground as his hands clutch at thin air. That one step toward us was a step too far, and now he's supine on the floor.

Down, but not out, the man screeches and cusses as he punches at my dog. Rufus bites, his big jaw clamping down on the man's right arm to hold him in place and neutralize the threat.

An ungodly howl issues from the intruder's mouth, and panic fills his eyes as he looks at where Rufus has him. I see what he sees there too: blood.

"Release," I command, and Rufus follows my order. The moment he unlatches his jaw from the guy's arm I realize we have a new problem. This isn't just a little bit of blood. It's a *lot* of blood.

Panicking now, the man hugs his arm to his chest, but a pool of red is spreading around him, growing wider with each pump of his heart. I kneel and move his arm so I can get a better look at the injury. It appears that Rufus's teeth punctured the man's brachial artery, and if he's not treated quickly, he'll bleed to death.

I need to call 911 and get some help here as soon as possible. Jumping to my feet, the knees of my pajama pants are wet with blood and stick to my legs as I search my pockets, hunting for my phone. Shit. No phone. I must have left it upstairs. Okay, I'll use the front desk phone, but first I need to stanch the bleeding.

Now I'm the one rummaging through the supply cabinets, coming up with a dog hemostasis strap. I fall to my knees beside the man again and try to fish the strap over his hand and up his arm. He struggles like he wants to get away, eyeing me with distrust and flinging blood around with each move he makes.

"Stay still," I grit through my teeth, "I need to stop the bleeding, or you'll die."

His distrust turns to pure panic, but he stops struggling and allows me to get the strap up his arm and tightened, a makeshift tourniquet to slow the bleeding.

"There," I say and try to smile at my patient, then jump to my feet again. Commanding Rufus to stay put, I run out to the front office. My bare feet slap the linoleum and crunch over broken glass as I make a mad dash for the phone. In my haste, I knock the front desk computer monitor onto the floor with a crash, but finally, I have the phone in my hands.

"911, what's your emergency?"

CHAPTER 25
ADAM

Probie claims his lasagna is orgasmic. I'm tempted to believe him, considering the savory aroma that fills the station. If this meal tastes half as good as it smells, I might stop giving Probie such a hard time about the way he folds laundry.

It's been a slow shift. We're sitting at the table in the mess room, playing cards and talking about Halloween costume ideas, when my mom calls. My family knows not to call me when I'm on shift unless it's an emergency, so I fold my cards and answer as I wander down the hallway toward the quiet of the bunk rooms.

"I know you're working. I won't keep you." Mom starts, then launches into a breathless monologue. "But I thought you'd like to know that Markus came by and picked up Rufus a little while ago. He looked tired. I asked about his father. He said that he passed away around one o'clock this morning. Didn't want to ask why he's back here so soon after the passing, but I could tell he's feeling sad and maybe a bit confused and exhausted. Also, he's not wearing a bandage over his stitches anymore. The injury looks good, no swelling or redness. I offered to feed him dinner, but he was in a rush to get his dog and leave. He's probably an introvert, and socializing is exhausting for him, so he needs a bit of a rest."

"Jesus, Mom, are you going to write his unauthorized biography next?"

"I just thought you'd want to know that he's back in town."

"Yes, thank you for the update," I say, and I mean it.

But I'm not sure what to do with the information. Last night, Markus called me and told me he liked me; then he hung up. It felt a bit odd at the time, but now, given the timeline my mom just relayed, I'm pretty sure that's when his father died. Jesus, how screwed up is that?

While he was suffering through a night of trauma and loss, I was obsessed with ideas of him and the future: a future *with* him, a future with him *in my bed*. That last notion really blows my mind. I've never been with a partner more than once. Not that I've made it a hard-and-fast rule to never explore a second date with my one-night stands. I just haven't. But with Markus, I want to *explore* everything.

I like him—a lot. I like his friendship and the sound of his laughter; the way he says "good boy" to Rufus and how I *want* him to say it to me; the way he tastes when he's wet from the rain; and the way he moans and tangles his fingers in my hair when I take his cock to the back of my throat. Whoops, there I go again, so consumed by thoughts of Markus that I haven't listened to a word my mom has said.

But I perk up when there's a commotion on Mom's end of the phone call. Through the static of the line, Alice—who's over at Mom's so much since the baby came, you'd think she moved back in —shouts at my Mom, "Someone stuffed six hundred dollars cash into the kennel donation box out by the road!"

"What?" My mom's reaction is so loud I hold the phone away from my ear, carefully pulling it back when she asks my sister, "Did they leave a note? Any explanation?"

"No. Nothing."

I don't need a note to know exactly who left that donation and exactly why they left it. I challenged Markus to donate the money he tried to pay me for taking him up to Mineral Wells, and he did.

Gah! As if I needed another reason to like this guy. He's a fantasy come true, Prince Charming from a fairytale. Does that make me Snow White, the lover he brought back to life with a kiss?

Overhead, the station's emergency alert system chimes, and a robotic voice reads the call details: "Attention Engine Thirty-one, Attention Medic Five, Attention Medic Three, respond to 202 North Main Street. Caller indicates robbery in progress, life-threatening injuries reported. Responders use caution."

Ice crackles through my veins, and I go completely numb. That's Markus's clinic. Someone has robbed it, and there are life-threatening injuries. Is it Markus? Is he hurt? Fear twists my stomach in knots, and the helplessness of separation forms a gnawing ache in the center of my chest.

I need to be there. *Now.*

Mom heard the emergency call through the phone, and she's barking orders to my sisters and brother-in-law as I hang up and run for the truck bay. The big door trundles open as I climb up into the driver's seat, impatient for the rest of the crew to join me. Probie is the last one out the door, having to make sure the lasagna doesn't burn in the oven while we're out.

As soon as he's in the truck and everyone's doors are closed, I hit the gas, Dee hits the siren, and we take off, racing downtown. The station is not far from Main Street, but the drive over feels like miles and miles. With each strobe of the red and white emergency lights, my mind flashes through nightmare scenarios of Markus lying on the floor of his clinic, injured or worse.

We arrive at the same time as Medic 5, and I pull to a stop behind my sister's sheriff's vehicle. Terrific, as if I don't have enough to worry about, now I know Ava is in there, too, probably with her gun drawn.

Seeming to read my mind, Drew offers from the back, "I'll chock the wheels. Go!"

With a quick glance over my shoulder, I silently thank him, then look to Dee. As the officer in charge of the scene, it's her call. She nods, giving me clearance to run inside. So I do, springing myself loose of the truck and sprinting for the building.

Shattered glass from the broken front door covers the clinic floor, and I squeeze through the hole to move inside, glass crunching under my boots as I step into the dark space. I find absolute chaos. One of the front desk computers lies sideways on the floor, the monitor shattered. Beside it a phone is tangled in its cord, a busy signal sounding from the receiver. And all around are bloody footprints.

My panic ratchets up as I follow the blood trail to the back of the building, where I hear voices. One of the voices belongs to my sister as she instructs, "Lie still so you don't bleed out."

I practically dive for the door, then come up short when I step inside and see all the blood. Arterial blood dots one wall, and a large pool of red ringed by a frenzy of bloody footsteps mars the floor in a gory mess. It smells gory, too, the strong copper stench of blood blending with the acrid smell of floor cleaner.

Lying supine in the center of it all is a man I do not recognize. My sister is on her knees beside him, checking his pupils and pulse as he hollers and writhes in pain. From behind me, Probie and one of the medics run to his aid.

I'm stunned, just staring at it all, trying to understand what I'm seeing. A dog snorts and grumbles behind me, and I turn to find Markus sitting on one of the supply shelves. Rufus stands at attention, cautiously watching everyone from beside his person.

Without thinking, I go to them. Only two strides separate us as I look them up and down. They paint a strange image, a tableau of horror and love. Markus has his hand on Rufus's head, sweetly petting his dog, who has blood dripping from his jowls. There's blood on Markus, too, covering his pajama pants and splattering across his white undershirt, but none of it appears to be from any wound on him. Still, I check, running my hands over his arms, his torso, his face.

Markus reaches for me, too, his palm shaking as he cups my cheek. I turn my gaze to his, and everything stops. Every single thing just *stops* as I stare into his big blue eyes.

He's okay. Thank God he's okay.

All the panic, all that maddening fear flushes out of me, and in my relief to see him alive and uninjured, I kiss him. But this is more than a kiss, so much *more*. When my lips meet Markus's, it's a statement, a promise. There is already something more between us—I know we both feel it—and this kiss is my first step toward exploring that.

When he angles his mouth against mine and parts his lips, I feel the promise in his kiss too. I groan and wrap an arm around his waist, taking more from the kiss, more from him, taking anything and everything he'll give me in this moment. I revel in the taste of him, sweet and clean, like candy and mouthwash.

He hasn't shaved today, and his stubble against my cheeks feels divine, tiny pricks of such sweet pain that bring my focus to his mouth's softness. And his hand, still touching my cheek, curls around the back of my neck to hold me close, to take from me just as I take from him. Sharing our strength, until we are so much stronger together.

When we slowly pull apart, I rest my forehead against his, and in a whisper, only meant for his ears, I say, "I was so worried."

Markus's eyes open to look deep into mine. "I'm fine, never better. Rufus saved me."

"Good boy," I say with a head scratch and a big smile at the dog, who sort of smiles back.

It's only then that I remember I'm on the job in a blood-soaked room full of people—including my sister and my entire crew.

I look over at the bleeding man on the floor, where Drew and one of the paramedics are securing him for transport to the emergency room. Dee is on her radio informing the hospital of their incoming patient while Probie is helping the other paramedic maneuver a stretcher through the door.

No one says a thing about my very unprofessional dalliance in the corner of a crime scene with the crime victim, but I'm not so naïve to think they didn't notice. Stepping back a bit, I take a longer look at Markus and ask, "Are you injured?"

"Just my feet."

With a quick glance down, I realize his feet are bare. I carefully lift one foot and then the other to inspect them, finding shards of glass in both. And, *shit*, in my haste to get in here and find Markus, I left my medic bag in the rig. Like she can read my mind, Dee sets it beside me.

I give her a grateful smile and nod, then get to work removing the glass and cleaning and bandaging his wounds.

Once he's taken care of, I turn my attention to Rufus, squatting in front of him to get a good look. I check his paws for glass, but he's fine, so I use some dog-safe wipes I found on the shelf to clean the man's blood off his snout, while Markus uses the wipes to clean his own hands.

As I do, my sister—Deputy Newman when she's in uniform—comes over to us, and I wonder aloud, "Am I tampering with evidence?"

"No, you're fine. I've taken some photos of the scene, so you can clean up." Now she turns to Markus. "Can you tell me what happened?"

"He came looking for drugs. Ketamine, I assume. Kept saying, 'You're not supposed to be here.' I guess word got out that the vet clinic was sitting empty with drugs inside."

"Jesus," I mutter.

Ava nods, then smirks at Rufus and scratches his head. "I s'pose now word will spread about this good boy here. No one's likely to bother you again with him on guard duty. For tonight, we'll board up the door so no one else gets any bright ideas."

I spot a pair of Crocs in a corner of the room and bring them to Markus, who gratefully slides them on so we can walk out over the glass. As for Rufus, I check that the dog is not harboring any residual aggression before I pick him up, all ninety pounds of him, and carry him over the glass and out of the clinic toward the waiting vehicles.

While we were inside rendering aide, apparently my mom has been organizing help too.

Gary and Clint, my brothers-in-law, stand by with cordless drills and a couple sheets of fresh plywood, waiting for us to clear the scene so they can board up the clinic overnight. And my sister Anna is sweeping glass off the pavement.

Once we've safely passed all the damage to the door, I set Rufus down, and he immediately goes to Markus's side, leaning into his legs as if to help prop his person up. Markus does look a bit unsteady, and his hands tremble, so I make him sit on the bumper of Gary's truck.

Initially, I fear he's showing signs of shock as he stares wide-eyed at everyone around him. But when he says, "They're all here to help?" I realize his "shock" is actually surprise at seeing this community stand up for him.

My chest fills with love and gratitude for my family. I could absolutely kiss every single one of them for showing up here to make Markus feel welcome, even as he reels from the stress and horror of this night…hell, this whole week!

Markus needs a place to feel safe, a place to call home. And my family has come here to give that to him.

Reading Markus's staring gaze as shock, too, a paramedic I don't really know comes to check his pupil response and look over the bandaging I put on his feet. Then he suggests to Markus, "I'd like to take you to the hospital to make sure you're okay."

Markus snaps out of his awestruck peace and shakes his head emphatically. The sudden movement looks like it might tip him over. A few of us reach out, as if we're going to hold him upright, and he tries to convince the paramedic. "I'm okay. I…I think I'm just hungry."

Hungry? After all *this*?

He adds, "I can't remember eating today."

Shit. We need to get this man a meal, STAT!

The paramedic frowns, like he wants to argue. Out of the corner of my eye, my mom looks like she's about to speak up, probably with an offer to cook Markus a meal. But Probie surprises us all when he says, "I made lasagna. Back at the station. There's plenty, enough for you to join us, Markus. We can make sure you're okay."

Everyone stares at Probie like he's sprouted a second head, and he hesitates, "Oh. Shit. Is that against policy or—"

"No, it's fine," Dee says, and warmth washes through me in waves. My team, my family—they're coming through for me, for Markus when he needs it, and I could cry with how good that feels.

Until tonight, I never even kissed a man in this town. Afraid, for some unfounded reason, that it would push the town's tolerance of who I am too far. Instead, not only are they accepting me and the kiss I planted on a man at a crime scene, but also they're accepting that man too.

It's like an earthquake, something that shifts oceans and continents inside me, opens up cracks and fissures of happiness, freedom, joy. I didn't know how this town truly felt about me until right now, and their acceptance is so much more than I could have hoped for. It's everything.

I always assumed hosting civilians to dinner at the fire station was a department policy violation, but no one seems to balk when Knox invites me and my man-eating dog to join them.

It's a wild ride back to the station in the back seat of Engine 31. I sit in the center, where I have a great view out the front window. Adam drives and Dee is in shotgun, while Knox and Drew sit in the back with me, and Rufus is in one of the jump seats at Drew's feet, being a very good boy as we go through yet another new and strange experience tonight.

Drew shows me where to find my seatbelt, and he hands me a pair of headphones with an attached microphone, so I can listen to the team chat as we ride the few blocks back to their station.

I enjoy the casual banter as Dee gives Knox a hard time, calling him Probie and asking what temp he left the lasagna on to warm while they were away on the call to my clinic. The normalcy of their conversation is a soothing relief after the screwed-up day I've had.

When we arrive at the station, Knox gets out and waves his arms to direct Adam as he backs into the garage bay, making sure he doesn't rear-end any of the exercise equipment they've fit into the space.

Coming down from the truck is quite a step. Rufus leaps out, no problem, but I take my time and use the handlebar beside the door to land carefully on my injured feet. Once I'm safely on the ground, I find that Rufus has been waiting for me. He leans into my legs again as he works like my guide dog, and we follow the crew inside.

I've never been in a fire station before, and I'm not sure what to expect, so I just take it all in as we step through the door from the truck bay into the kitchen. My first impression: I thought it would be bigger. The kitchen isn't much larger than what might be found in an average home, with a standard set up of appliances and cabinetry. Beyond the kitchen is a dining area, filled with one very large table that can seat about ten, I'd guess. Past the dining table is a rec room with two sectional sofas, a large television, and some dart boards on the far wall.

Off to one side is an entrance to a utility space with a laundry facility, and on the other end of the room, a hallway leads away, I assume toward the bunk rooms. I don't know why I expected this place to smell like a high school locker room, but it smells scrumptious, thanks to the warming lasagna, I assume. My stomach rumbles; I'm starved. But first—

"This is the men's locker room," Adam says, like he's reading my mind, and he points to one of the two doors that open off the laundry facility space. "Feel free to shower and change. I'll keep Rufus entertained."

I smile at him in gratitude and tug my backpack a little higher on my shoulder as I go into the shower room. Discarding my soiled clothes as hazmat, I rush to get under the spray of hot water and wash the stranger's blood off me. Finally, as the steamy heat eases my tense muscles, I take deep breaths of the damp air and start to relax.

Everything in me hurts. My muscles are sore from holding me upright for the past week as I survived and survived and survived again. From the car accident to the trip home to the robbery, I've been coiled tight and pumped full of adrenaline more than is probably healthy. Now, as all that tension washes out of me, swirling down the drain with someone else's blood, I feel beat, exhausted.

When I'm as clean as I can get, my skin pink and angry from the vigorous scrubbing, I dry and change into a new pair of scrubs and a tee. I apply fresh bandages to the wounds on my feet, and rinse off my Crocs before slipping them back on. Then I head out to the dining area.

God the smell. Pretty sure I consume a few hundred calories with each inhale of the scrumptious aroma. Knox is cutting the lasagna into sections and serving it onto each person's plate. I arrive just in time to watch him scoop up a big serving and pull it loose from the casserole dish; the cheese stretches in long strings until it lets go, and he sets a big square in front of me.

Without a word, Adam sets a bowl of what looks like Pralines 'n Cream ice cream beside my plate, then walks away. When he returns a moment later, he sets down two glasses of water, one for me and one for himself as he takes the seat beside me.

"What's this?" I ask about the bowl of ice cream. From the look of it, I'm the only one with this side dish.

He glances at me as he licks the tip of his thumb, like he got some ice cream there as he was dishing it up. "You like to eat sweets before savory, and I figured if any day called for dessert before dinner, this is that day."

I'm surprised he remembered my habit. My mother was the only other person who paid attention to my sweet tooth, and she never stopped giving me grief about it. During meals, she'd fill my plate with too much meat and vegetables, then withhold dessert until I cleaned my plate. At my first dinner at boarding school, I realized I had the power to decide my portion sizes and the order in which I ate them. I've started with dessert ever since.

I smile at Adam and chuckle a bit, and I think it's the first time I've used my humor muscles since seeing my father in his death bed. "Thank you," I tell him, and he smiles, too, that dimple in his cheek almost enough to distract me from my food.

Almost.

Without waiting for anyone else to start eating or say grace—my mother would be horrified by my bad manners—I take a bite of the confection and nearly faint at the taste of it. The sugary cream melts on my tongue and runs down my throat in sweet goodness.

Everything around me vanishes, just for a few moments while I experience this meal: a perfect bowl of ice cream followed by the hearty goodness of Knox's lasagna, which somehow manages to taste better than it smells.

Is this heaven? Maybe I died in that car accident, and these past few days were my purgatory as I found my way here. *Jesus, I'm losing my mind.*

I take a big gulp of water and don't stop there, drinking the whole glass down in a matter of seconds. Adam gets up to pour me another, and I drink that one down, too, so he brings a third. Trying to be courteous, I thank him each time between bites of food until my plate is clean and my stomach is full and roiling, making me decline seconds. Sitting back in my chair, I reach for Rufus so I can pet his head and shoulders as I enjoy the spirited debate about Halloween costume ideas as everyone else eats. Yes, I think this is heaven, and the best part is, I'm pretty sure I'm not dead.

After dinner, Adam offers to let me rest in one of their bunk rooms, but this isn't a hotel, and they don't need to wait on me, so I settle onto one of the couches, Rufus at my feet, and watch a movie with the crew. It's some old Patrick Swayze and Keanu Reeves movie that Drew insists I need to see. Everyone else groans—apparently they've seen it a lot. It seems like a good flick, but I only half watch as my eyes droop between each blink, and my head feels increasingly heavy on my shoulders.

Daylight streams through the windows beside the couch when I open my eyes again. Did I fall asleep in the middle of the movie? Glancing around, I find myself alone in the rec room, a blanket draped over me. Rufus whines, and I sit up so I can pet him where he still sits beside my feet, like he's still on high alert, still protecting me.

"You're such a good boy," I whisper to him as I scratch behind his ears and kiss the top of his head.

Standing, I fold the blanket and set it aside as I stretch and yawn. Everything hurts. I twist, and my back pops, but it all still hurts. Shuffling on my aching feet, I go into the kitchen where a pot of coffee has started to brew. In this moment, when it's just Rufus and me and the steady drip, drip, drip of the coffee maker, it's too quiet, and the quiet unsettles me.

Except… Wait, there's another sound. It's a steady rhythmic beat, like the coffee drip, only metallic, a banging noise. And it's coming from the other side of the door leading into the garage. I hobble on my wounded feet over to peer out the window in the door, and there I see the source of the sounds—weights clanking together.

In an instant, I recognize the shirtless man working out. Adam has his back to the door as he performs a set of cable curls with an impressive amount of weight. I watch him, mesmerized by the shifting muscles of his arms, back, and shoulders as he lifts and lowers the weights.

His skin glistens with sweat, and the sight makes my fingers twitch to touch him and my mouth water to taste him. Has it only been two nights since we were together? It feels like a lifetime ago.

When Adam reaches the end of his set, he lets the weights go with a final clang and turns to grab his towel from a bench. He notices me watching him and freezes, staring back at me like he's waiting for me to make a move, do something, say something. There's so much that's been left unsaid between us, I wouldn't even know where to start.

Well, I start by pushing the door open and limping out to where he is. He quickly wipes the bench off with his towel and gestures for me to sit there, so I do. Rufus, seeming to consider me safe with Adam, walks past us and out to the front lawn to relieve himself.

Adam slips a T-shirt on over his sweaty torso and sits beside me. Then he quickly jumps up. "Sorry, I probably stink."

"No!" I argue too quickly, too loudly. "You smell"—amazing, mouthwatering—"fine."

Slowly, he sits again, putting a little more space between us this time.

We sit there, side by side, each staring at our feet and the pavement beneath. It's absurd that we can't just talk to each other. I have so many things I want to tell him, ask him, and yet when he's near, I just stare and grin and fawn like a teenage boy amid his first crush.

When the silence has stretched far too long, I realize I need to say something. I did interrupt his workout after all, and surely I did that for a reason.

"I'm sorry—" I say.

"I'm sorry—" he says at the same time.

We both glance up, staring at one another, not sure who should speak first.

He's the first to try again, asking, "Why are *you* sorry?"

Oh, I thought that would be obvious. "Because I was an asshole to you in Mineral Wells. I treated you terribly, and I'm so sorry. I was blaming you for things that aren't your fault."

"Oh." He sort of chuckles and shakes his head. "Markus, you were going through a lot of shit. And, I'm sorry, too, about that night. I shouldn't have…we shouldn't have had sex."

Wait. What? "Why not?"

"Because you were in a bad place, and maybe you weren't thinking clearly. And then again last night, when I kissed you… I absolutely should not have done that, and I'm so sorry."

"You regret it?"

"No!" His eyes dart up to mine, and he shakes his head. "No. I don't… It's just… I shouldn't have kissed you without your consent, especially in front of other people. I don't know if you're out or not, and I just kissed you in front of everyone like I had the right to do that when I didn't, and I'm sorry."

"Oh. Well… I don't regret it either."

His expression changes in an instant, from pensive worry to ecstatic relief. And, God, that's a sexy look on him. His eyes seem to darken, his pupils expanding as his gaze moves from my eyes to my mouth and back.

"You don't?" he asks in a breathy tone.

"I don't." I sound breathy too.

"Thank God," he says as he shifts on the bench, erasing any distance between us as he lifts his hands to cup my face. His lips are practically touching mine when he asks, "May I kiss you again?"

The question, the fact that he asked it, is so charming, I'm rendered practically speechless. I nod, an emphatic yes, and finally manage to use my words too. "Yes. Please."

This time, when we kiss, it's sweet and slow, not starved and desperate like the times before; not tinged with the stench of musty motel curtains or the tang of arterial blood splatter. This time, it's just him and me, and it's perfect.

All the anxiety I've carried since that first time we made love seeps out of me. I grab him, desperate to hold on, and fist my hands in his shirt, pulling him closer, so close he's pretty much on top of me on the weight bench. He's hard and growing harder in those loose workout shorts. I'm hard, too, so damn ready for him.

Just as I'm starting to wonder what the firehouse policy is regarding fucking members of the community in the truck bay, Adam pulls away. Looking kiss drunk and huffing deep breaths in and out as he presses his forehead to mine, he whispers, "When my shift ends, come home with me. I know there's a lot going on, but I need you."

That's a hell of an invitation, and Adam's rough voice as he extends it sends shivers down my spine. I sound far less seductive when I awkwardly squawk, "Yes."

Rufus's nails click and clack against the garage pavement as he comes to sit before us, staring as we share this moment. Adam's lips twitch and turn up into a grin as we both laugh at my dog.

Markus and Rufus explore my home, and I watch to see what captures their attention. Rufus mostly follows Drusilla around, sniffing everything. I'm glad we stopped at Mom's kennel to pick her up—it gives Rufus a friend to focus on, while I focus on every move Markus makes.

Despite his injured feet, Markus is still standing, looking closely at the photos I framed and hung on the wall. Some show me and the rest of the Krause Fire Department team when we placed second in the Texas Firefighting Challenge. We were sweaty and exhausted and smiling with pride at our accomplishment. Others are family photos: Mom, my sisters, and I celebrating Christmas or riding horses at my uncle's ranch.

I'd love to let him explore every room, see the things that matter to me, but I don't have the patience for all of that, not now. I'm tired and horny, and there is one cure for both ailments: my bed.

Approaching from behind him, I rest my mouth on his neck, tasting his skin with the tip of my tongue, breathing in his scent. He turns and his bright blue eyes capture my undivided attention, hypnotizing me as his hands reach out, his touch so soft against my waist it nearly tickles.

I want him so badly it doesn't feel like *want* anymore. This is a *need* now, a need so intense it's bordering on desperation, a gnawing hunger I must feed before it consumes me. But I wait.

His need must be as desperate as mine, because he growls like a beast when he clasps his fingers around the back of my neck and pulls me in for a deep kiss. Now I'm the one growling as I mold my body against his, my cock so hard it hurts.

Steering blindly around furniture and through doorways, I move us into my bedroom, kicking the door shut behind us. It's like we're dancing, all the way into bed.

Markus laughs when we fall onto the mattress, landing in a tangle of limbs. We undress in a tangle of limbs, too, our clothes tying us in knots that have us breaking the kiss to laugh. I like it, that little pause for levity. Wanting to slow things down, I pull away, far enough that I can finish undressing as he does the same.

Once we're both naked, he takes over, pushing me onto my back and rising up over me to give me a lascivious grin as he kisses his way down my body. When he takes me in his mouth, I holler from the hot heat and groan as his tongue teases the tip of my cock before he sucks me to the back of his throat.

Then he fists my erection, stroking a few times as he releases me from his mouth and asks, "Have you always been a top?"

I'm not expecting any conversation beyond a bit of dirty talk, so I have to concentrate to answer, piecing his words into clear thoughts. He distracts me, licking the tip of my cock, swirling his tongue through the pre-cum that beads there.

"Um," I struggle to breathe, let alone speak when he does that, but manage, "Since the first time, yeah."

"Didn't like being a bottom?"

"Not a fan." I nearly scream that last word, and my back arches off the bed when he sucks me to the back of his throat again. God, his masterful mouth has me way too close to coming.

"What if I could make it feel really good for you?" he asks, and I crane my neck to stare at him.

Is he asking… "Do you want to switch?"

That devilish tongue twirls my length again and I'm tempted, very tempted to say fuck it and let him fuck me any way and every way he wants. I mean, what's holding me back?

My first time doesn't compare to this. I didn't have a clue what I was doing and neither did my partner. Since then, I've always topped, but can I open my mind—and body—to what he's asking?

Instead of answering me, Markus peppers me with kisses as he makes his way back up to take my mouth again. This slow pace has me so turned on, wound tight, and desperate for more. I reach for his cock, stroking his length with my fist as he jerks me with the same rhythm. Pulling his mouth from mine, he nibbles my bottom lip and then my jaw as he whispers, "I want to fuck you, Adam. Will you let me?"

"Yes, please." I don't just agree to his proposition, I beg for it. Any hesitation I might have felt with another man just isn't there with Markus. I need his cock inside me like I need my next breath. As if he can read my mind, he obliges, rearranging himself on the bed so his cock is at my mouth just as he takes mine to the back of his throat again.

I fist the base of his length and suck him deep. He mirrors my movements, swallowing me whole just as I do the same to him. God, it feels so good, so exciting when we're synced like this.

I didn't notice Markus reach for the lube I set on the bedside table, but soon I feel a cool, wet finger teasing my entrance. With a deep breath, I try to relax as he slowly pushes the digit inside.

"Oh fuck!" The sensation makes me gasp and huff. He pauses to give me a moment to adjust. But it's only a moment before he pushes deeper, exploring my tight hole in slow, shallow strokes that get faster and longer each time he takes my length to the back of his throat. Jesus, it feels strange, but…*good*. So good that soon I'm writhing and clutching the globes of his ass as I moan around his cock.

With the way he's teasing and sucking me, I almost don't realize he's pushed a second finger in to join the first. Almost. "Oh Jesus, fuck!" I exclaim as I try to take in this new fullness. He chuckles, and I feel that vibration all the way up my spine.

Markus carefully pushes a third finger inside me, and the sensation is so overwhelming, my body doesn't know what to make of it. This feels like it could hurt, like it *should* hurt, but the way he's doing this… *nothing* hurts.

It feels amazing and this is just his fingers. I want more. Suddenly, I'm desperate to have him inside me. I pull my mouth off his cock so I can beg. "Markus, I need you to fuck me."

He doesn't argue or waste a single moment; he tosses one of the condom packets to me, and I know he's asking me to put it on him. When I have him sheathed, he gets on his knees and gently pulls his fingers out of my ass. I move to roll over, so he can take me from behind, but he stops me, pressing my shoulders down against the mattress as he settles himself between my legs.

I blink up at him, a little surprised. I've never fucked anyone like this. I'm not sure what to do with my legs, but Markus arranges me how he wants me. I let him lead, and when the head of his cock presses inside I try to keep breathing as I take it.

Christ, it's so *much*. Pleasure and pain and everything in between.

Again, he's careful to let me adjust, but soon, slow and steady, he pushes deeper with each stroke until he's all the way inside. God, it's intense. He's so big. I grit my teeth to keep from screaming. I don't know if I would scream for him to stop or beg him to fuck me until I come all over our chests. This intensity is so *much*, my mind is lost to the sensations.

I'm much more vocal when I'm getting fucked than I am when I'm the one doing the fucking. Markus seems to delight in the sounds of my pleasure, hovering his lips so close to mine that he could kiss me, but he doesn't want to silence my groans and gasps.

I like the sounds Markus makes, too, concentrated huffs, like he's holding back, trying to stay steady, even as the basest part of him wants to go wild. I clutch his ass and squeeze, wanting so badly for him to go wild along with me.

Between us, my cock is hard as stone and rubs against Markus's stomach, my pre-cum getting him all wet. He shifts his hips so he can fuck me hard and deep, and he takes my cock in his hand to jerk me off with the same rhythm.

"Oh my God." I grab onto him, desperately grasping at his arms and back and ass as I yell, "Fuck! Yes, Markus, yes!'

Spurred by my words, he fucks me faster, jerks me harder, and for the first time since this started, he speaks. "You like that, babe? You like the way I fuck you?"

"Yes!"

Markus stares down at where we join together, groaning as he clasps a hand on my knee to control our rhythm. "Look how good you take my cock."

Swear to Christ, one more word like that out of him, and I will come into next week.

I take over jerking myself off so he can use both hands for leverage as he pistons his hips hard and fast. We're fucking so rough that this old bed bangs into the wall in a rhythm to match ours, and the sound is so fucking erotic.

Even more erotic is the growly bite to Markus's words when he says, "I need you to come first. Come for me, babe."

Like I'm following orders, my body does exactly that. From deep down inside, ecstasy takes hold and rolls through me in a churning wave until I shout and spasm, and my cock shoots hot streams of cum on both our chests. The moment Markus sees me come, he presses deep and hard inside me and bellows as he orgasms as well.

Well. Damn. That was absolutely, without a doubt the best sex of my life.

Markus is gentle now, careful as he pulls out slowly and collapses onto the bed beside me. I stretch my legs and turn onto my side to stare at him as he does the same. Now, when we kiss, it's not about sex and heat and feral desire. This kiss is soft and sweet and soothing. And when we come apart, we grin at each other like we're sharing some secret.

Markus looks down between us and touches his chest, where he finds the wetness of my ejaculation and spreads it around. I trace my fingers through the wetness, too, then explore the ridges of his muscles and tease his still-hard nipples in tight circles.

"Thank you," Markus says.

"For sex?"

He chuckles. "Well, thank you for that, too, but mostly thank you for trusting me."

I consider those words, wondering if that's what it is I'm feeling. Is this euphoric emotion trust? Do I trust him? After only a moment's consideration, I know without a doubt, the answer is yes. Why? I don't know.

Hell, I hardly know Markus. I don't know his birthday or his middle name or if he wears socks to sleep like I do. But for the first time in my life, I look across the pillow at my lover, and I *want* to know everything about him, want to share everything about me.

"I'm sorry about last time." Markus's apology interrupts my thoughts. "When I got pissy with you…after. It wasn't fair to you. I'm not used to casual sex. I'd never had a one-night stand before."

Chuckling, I tweak his nipple as I inform him: "Newsflash, babe. You still haven't had a one-night stand." It's only after I've said it that I realize I just used the same term of endearment he used when we were having sex. I like the sound of it, and I like the fact that Markus has broken every unwritten rule I have regarding relationships. "You're the only person I've ever been with more than once, and you're the first person I've ever been with in this bed. Hell, I've never even had sex in this county before you."

A laugh bursts out of Markus, but when he sees I'm not joking, he frowns. "Really?"

I nod.

"Why?"

My defensive instincts have me wanting to change the subject. This isn't something I talk about. Everyone in this gossipy little town already knows. But Markus is new here, so I take the time to explain. "My family."

"Your family seems very supportive."

"My mom and my sisters are amazing, but they're not my entire family. Back when I was eight…" God, I don't even know where to start. So I guess I'll start at the beginning. "My dad always wanted a son, and after three daughters, he finally got his wish with me. But I wasn't the *right* kind of son for him. I embarrassed him. He would harp on me when I did anything remotely 'girly,' so we would play our 'girly' games when he was out.

"One summer afternoon, my sisters and I had all dressed up and teased out our hair, and we had RuPaul's *Supermodel* song playing as we strutted the runway through the hall and into the kitchen. I was doing my turn to the left and right when Dad got home from work.

"He flipped out, and he hit me…and he kept hitting me. My sisters tried to intervene, but he wouldn't stop. Ava ran out to the kennels to get Mom. He was so out of control that Mom had to pull a gun on him to get him to stop hurting me.

"I was out of it at that point, curled into a ball on the floor, so I didn't see it, but they told me later that she yelled at him to leave and never come back or she'd shoot him full of holes."

"They defended you," Markus says.

"They did." I grin a little and nod. "Mom called the sheriff, pressed assault charges. She also hired a divorce lawyer the next day." I take in a deep breath and let it out, then I voice an emotion I've never truly acknowledged before. "The women in my life are amazing, and I feel very lucky to have them, but I also feel very guilty."

"Why?"

"Because I'm the reason we're not a full family anymore. My mom doesn't have a husband, and my sisters don't have a dad because of who I am. When Alice got married a few years ago, I'm the one who walked her down the aisle, and it made me feel bad that she didn't have her father to do that…because of me."

"Sit up," Markus commands, as he does the same, scooting back to lean against the headboard as he stares at me. I raise a brow at the command but do as I'm told and face him.

"You're not to blame." Markus's tone brooks no argument. "Your dad's shitty behavior is not your fault. You did nothing wrong."

Markus is good at this emotional-support stuff, and it's appreciated. Still… "Intellectually, I know you're right, but it doesn't stop me from carrying the guilt. Since that day, I've strived to be the perfect son, perfect brother. I want to make my family proud because I feel like I owe them for choosing me over him." Chuckling a little with embarrassment, I get to the point of this entire story. "That's why I've never dated in Krause."

Markus frowns.

With a shrug, I explain. "I lost my virginity at football camp in San Antonio, senior year of high school. I loved it… Well, I didn't love going without lube, but I loved everything else about that experience. Finally, I truly knew who I was and what I wanted in my life. The thing is, I equated the peace of that revelation to the freedom that came with being out of town, away from all the baggage and expectations of the people I love. So ever since that experience, I've traveled to…date. Until you."

He smiles and so do I. He moves his hand toward me, and I take it, lacing our fingers together.

"So now what?" He asks.

I shrug. "I don't know. I'm a bit scared."

"Why?"

"Because, as progressive as this little town tries to be for me, I don't want to push that limit. In fact, last night at your clinic—"

"When you kissed me in front of everyone?"

I chuckle and nod. "Yes. That was a first for me and this town. Krause knows me and loves me as their friendly neighborhood gay firefighter, but they've never seen me kiss a man until you."

"So you kind of came out last night too."

I nod. "I guess I did."

"Do you regret it?"

I consider the implications and ramifications of that kiss, the gossip and wagging tongues, and none of that matters as much as how special it felt to me. The answer is clear. "No, not at all. Do you?"

"Not at all," Markus says with a small smile, adding, "I've always been out."

"Really?" Considering his reaction to returning to his hometown, I assumed he was dealing with the same turmoil as me.

"When my parents sent me away to conversion therapy, that was hell. I wouldn't wish that on my worst enemy. But, after, when they sent me to boarding school, it was helpful for me to be away from them. It gave me the opportunity to learn about myself. I knew I never wanted to be the person my parents expected me to be, so instead I became…well, me. As for you, I think you're more out and open than you give yourself credit, I mean, Rooster Crows is hardly closeted."

How the hell… "You know about Rooster Crows?"

He gives me a cheeky grin. "Alice told me."

"She's trouble, that one."

"I'm going to enjoy working with her."

I groan, but it's a front. The idea of them talking about me at work is strangely exciting. But this also has me wondering, if he knows about Rooster Crows, if he's watched the channel, then… "What did you think about the most recent video?"

Markus frowns. "I didn't get a chance to watch. Why?"

I squeeze his hand in mine. "Driving home from Mineral Wells, I made a video asking my viewers for guidance. I needed to know what it meant to want *more* with a guy and want that *more* so badly your chest hurts."

His grin looks bashful, which is terribly charming. "Even after I was such a pissy jerk?"

"Even after that."

"And what did your viewers say?"

"That if I want *more*, I should take *more*. With consent, of course."

Markus raises a brow and chuckles. "And what does taking more entail?"

I pretend to ponder, but it's hardly a stretch of my imagination. Slowly, I lean in, and he angles closer, too, but not nearly enough, so I close the distance between us.

This kiss feels new somehow, which is interesting considering I've kissed him more than I've ever kissed anyone before. He darts his tongue out to take little tastes of my lips as I mold my mouth to his. With a groan, he melts into me, his body so hot as I press him back against my bed. But first, I ask, "Do I have your consent to take more?"

"Fuck, yes," he moans against my mouth. "My enthusiastic consent."

CHAPTER 28
MARKUS

Adam can cook. He explains that it's because they take turns cooking dinners at the station during their shifts. Why he's such a whiz in the kitchen is hardly important; all that matters to me right now is the French toast he made for a late breakfast. I glance at the clock—almost four in the afternoon. Correction— *very* late breakfast, but I don't care about that either.

I can't remember the last time I felt this relaxed and at peace. Spending time in Adam's bed today is exactly the sort of physical and mental therapy I need after the last few days.

I twirl a bit of the toast in a pool of syrup and look across the table at Adam. He's watching me with a relaxed and dreamy expression, which I imagine mirrors my own. This comfort I feel with him is new, like everything fits right when we're together.

After a moment of sharing that silent stare, he asks, "What?"

"Nothing," I say, but it's a lie. My mind races with, well, *everything*. Past, present, and future, happiness and sadness and everything in between. It all whirls around inside me, and it's a bit overwhelming.

But when I look at Adam, my mind calms, and my heart swells, and I feel fresh air in my lungs like it's the first breath I've taken in this life.

If I'm interpreting these feelings correctly, I think it means I like this guy. *A lot.* As Adam would say, I want *more* with him. It's an exciting prospect, and it's a bit terrifying too. New town, new car, new relationship, new me? That's a lot of newness. Am I ready for it all?

The look Adam gives me is cryptic, like he's trying to see into my head and read my mind, but soon enough he glances away at Rufus, who is curled up in a cuddle puddle with Drusilla.

"When should we admit it?"

"Admit what?"

"That they're a couple."

"Probably about the same time that you admit you've foster failed Drusilla and officially adopt her."

Adam's lips curl on one side in a cheeky smirk. "I've never failed at anything in my life."

I can't help but laugh whenever he looks at me like that. "Well, in that case, it's a foster win!"

Now he laughs. "I like the sound of that." He dips his head and lowers his tone to coo at the dog. "What do you think, Drusilla? Who's your daddy?"

That makes me laugh again, and it feels good. Being with him is nice and easy, and I hadn't realized how much I needed something nice and easy in my life.

At Adam's question, Drusilla gets to her feet and crosses to him, licking all over his chin when he moves his lips out of her reach. He scratches behind her ears and kisses the top of her head, and she pretty much melts from the attention.

"That looks like a yes to me," I say.

Now I coo at Drusilla when I ask her, "And who's your boo?"

"It's Rufie," Adam says in a syrupy voice.

"Rufie?" I cringe.

He looks at the ceiling as he reconsiders. Then he says, "Uh. Ew. No, that's a terrible nickname. We'll stick with Rufus."

"Good plan." I laugh once more. Jesus, do I ever laugh this much? Out of the blue, I start quizzing him, desperate for more information.

"When is your birthday?"

Raising a brow, Adam answers, "April twentieth. Yours?"

"September eleventh."

"Oh wow."

"Yeah, it's weird. What's your favorite color?"

He laughs and shrugs. "Red...no, blue. You?"

"Hmm. Green. Favorite food?"

Adam ponders the question for a moment, then excitedly answers, "There's this taco stand in San Antonio. I'll take you sometime. You've got to try their al pastor. Life changing."

Is he suggesting we travel to San Antonio together? Because it sounds like he's planning a date. And I like the sound of that. Even if we're not talking specifics, I like how easily the idea of us sharing things together comes to his mind. To keep from fixating on that notion, I ask a new question. "Do you always wear socks when you sleep?"

Adam laughs so hard he gets the dogs riled up. They circle his chair like they want in on the joke. He kicks a foot up, wiggling his toes in his Charlie Brown Christmas themed socks. "Yes. And if I had my druthers, I'd wear them when I'm having sex too."

Now I laugh, one of those laughs that clears the cobwebs from your mind and fills your chest with fresh air. "Uh, no. I'm going to have to veto that."

He smiles so wide I can see both dimples in his cheeks, and when he tries to quell the smile by biting his lip, my heart goes pitter-patter. Damn, this man is fine and funny and quirky, and I'm really, really into him. This time, I'm too distracted with his grin to come up with another question.

"Have I told you everything you want to know?" he finally asks me.

"For now."

"Well, then, let's get started."

Started?

Adam stands from the table and takes our plates to the sink. When he claps his hands, the dogs assemble attentively at his feet, but he addresses me when he speaks. "We'll shower, then head over to the clinic to help clean up."

Uh…what? "*Help* clean up?"

Adam nods as he reaches the door to his bedroom, making a show of pulling his socks off like he's doing a striptease, then he disappears inside. I follow him and the trail of discarded clothing, which leads me to his bathroom. Inside, I find him naked, warming up the water for a shower.

"What do you mean 'help clean up'? Who are we helping?"

"Everyone," Adam says casually over his shoulder, then he turns to face me. God he's gorgeous, especially when he's naked and rock hard, that erection pointed right at me. "Come here."

I forget whatever it was we were talking about and follow his command. Pushing down my boxer shorts until they fall to the floor, I walk into his arms and trace my fingers over his chest and down to his jutting cock.

Adam presses me to the shower wall, where the spray douses us both as he kisses me, and his hands rove to my length. I stroke him as he does the same to me and lose myself to the sensation of his touch, his taste. His kiss is maple-syrup sweet and nearly masks all the devilish things he's doing to my body.

When he pulls away, water drips from our hair and down our faces as we catch our breath. Adam comes closer, his whole body against mine, our cocks pressed together. I love the heat of it and how his silky texture is ribbed with thick veins. Between us, he links our fingers like we're shaking hands, but with our linked grip ringing our cocks.

Oh. Wow. I've never tried this before, but Adam guides my hand with his so we're jerking our cocks off together. And, God, it feels amazing.

He stares into my eyes as we fuck like this, the shower spray and our pre-cum making our strokes smooth and fast as we near the point of release. I don't think I've blinked this whole time, so entranced by his gaze as he guides the pace of our linked grip.

"Are you gonna come for me, babe?"

The rumbly sound of his deep voice when he calls me babe is music to my ears. It turns me on just as much as it fills my heart with warmth. I nod excitedly. "Yes. Oh God, yes."

With that, he squeezes our cocks harder, and I do too. The feel of us pressed so tight together is fucking amazing. When we each orgasm, our hot cum combines as it marks us both, a mutual claiming this time. He is mine, just as I am his. I know that now, without a doubt.

Once we've come down from that high, Adam bathes me. His fingers are gentle as he runs them through my hair and over my skin, such a contrast to the roughness from before. I bathe him, too, loving the way the soap suds cling to his skin like they're as desperate to touch him as I am.

Once we're rinsed and dried and dressed, I remember my question from before our steamy shower sex and ask him again, "What do you mean that everyone is helping clean up?"

Everyone, it turns out, is the entire town of Krause. Or at least that's how it seems. Adam parks his truck across Main Street, and I'm shocked by the sight that greets me when I look over at my clinic. The boards that Adam's brothers-in-law used to cover the broken door are off, so is the broken door, and three men work to install a new one.

I practically jump out of Adam's truck before he puts it in park and run over to the men to see what's going on. I recognize one of them easily—Knox County from Adam's fire crew—but the other two are strangers.

"What's up, Doc?" Knox says to me, and then we both frown. "Uh, yeah. Anyway, these are my brothers Briscoe and Clay."

I shake their hands, then look at the door they're installing. It's brand new, with a heavy-duty locking mechanism. "Where did this door come from?"

"Al's Hardware," Knox says and nods to an older man who's just stepped through the opening with a level in one hand and some shims in the other. "This is Al."

"Howdy," Al says.

"Nice to meet you, Al. How much do I owe you for the door?" I ask him.

"Aw, not much, Doc. Maybe a couple nail trims for my dog?"

Uh... I'm astounded. Not sure what to say. A couple nail trims would cost just thirty dollars. I'm certain this door costs far more than that, not to mention the labor for installation. Before I can argue or insist I pay him the full costs, Adam tugs at my arm to take me through the opening and into the lobby.

Worried about the dogs' paws, I check the floor for glass, but it's completely clean. Not only clear of glass but blood too.

Adam's mom and his sisters are here, as well as Dee and Drew from his fire crew, and a whole squad of other locals—some I recognize, some I don't—are cleaning and mopping my clinic. Even the elderly librarian who wrecked her car into mine is here, though she's leaning on a cane and wearing a neck brace, and everyone is encouraging her to sit down.

"What is happening?" I mutter to myself.

Adam must hear me because he says, "This town needs a vet."

"So?"

With a chuckle, he tells me, "*So*, they want to make sure you have everything you'll need to run this place safely."

I frown at him. "You knew about all of this?"

"Didn't know about the door—that's the County brothers' doing—but Alice and Mom organized a few locals to help with the cleanup, and that's my brother-in-law Clint up on the ladder installing the security camera. He also brought in the computer and phone."

Sure enough, all new devices sit in place of my broken computer and ancient phone at the front desk. And Clint stands on a ladder, adjusting a camera to face the door and windows.

Too stunned to do much of anything, I stare at all these people, these virtual strangers who've come here today to help me. But quickly, my mind moves out of that comfort zone as I stare down the hallway to where it all happened. I dread going back into that supply room, afraid to see the state of it. Have they cleaned that up too?

Hesitating only a moment, I walk that way. Adam follows, and so do the dogs, their claws clicking on the linoleum like a countdown toward that terrible space. I fortify myself for the bloodbath I expect to see. Instead, it's pristine. Someone—or several someones—has scrubbed the blood from every inch of the walls and floor. They straightened and cleaned the contents of my shelves and put it all back to right, like nothing ever happened here.

I'm so grateful I could cry. This community…my God. I don't even have words for how I feel right now. To be not just tolerated but *claimed* by a community is an experience I've never known. It feels so good and right, and… Fuck I think I might cry. Seeming to sense the vulnerability of my mood, Adam steps beside me and puts his arm around my waist.

"Thank you for this," I say once I've swallowed the lump in my throat.

"Don't thank me. I was with you the whole time, babe."

There's that term of endearment again. I really like it. "You organized it though."

"My sister organized it. You made a good decision hiring her," he says with a wink.

I stare at him a moment, that cheeky grin of his so mesmerizing, and a tidal wave of emotion swamps me. The urge to laugh and cry and kiss him all come at me at once. And I think I do laugh and cry as I pull him in for a kiss. We're in the same place where Adam kissed me amid a blood bath last night, but today it's serene, calm normalcy. And it's fucking fantastic.

Adam pulls away from the kiss and presses his forehead against mine, his arms cinched around my waist to hold me near as he says, "Last night, my mom had just told me you were back in town when we got the call out to this address. All I knew was a robbery was in progress and life-threatening injuries were reported. I was petrified it was you who was hurt. And the thought that kept screaming in my head as I raced over here was, 'I can't lose him, not when I've just found him.' Then I saw all the blood and—"

I kiss him, unable to wait another moment before my lips are on his, capturing his anguished words, and replacing them with that soft, sweet connection. When he kisses me back, his rigid body seems to melt into mine. I melt into him too. His kiss, his nearness give me strength, like I can balance better when he's around. It feels like I can rest some of my weight on his shoulders yet still stand tall.

"Enough of that, you two." Alice clamors into the supply room with one end of a file cabinet, her husband lugging the other end. "Listen, Boss Man, we're going to have to talk about grope sessions in the storage room. This could become a hostile work environment if I'm going to keep walking in on you making out with my wee tiny baby little brother."

"Could we chill with the adjectives, big *old* sister?" Adam retorts.

I chuckle at them both before asking the burning question, "Why are you bringing my file cabinet into the supply closet?"

Adam's sister nods at her husband to put his end down, and she sets the cabinet upright in the corner. "You don't need it anymore, so we're getting it out of the way. If you want to sell it, I know a guy—"

"Why won't I need a file cabinet anymore?"

"Because, lazy bones, while y'all were sleeping, I digitized your records with the new computer system Clint set up. You're welcome!"

Adam hooks his arm around his sister's neck and gives her head a noogie that messes up her hair. "There were definitely *bones* involved, Sis, but they weren't lazy."

"Ew, TMI. Boss! I need to file an HR complaint!"

"You are HR, Sis." Adam lets her go when she tickles his armpit.

"Well in that case, I'm giving myself a well-deserved raise!" Alice says this as she comes at me with a hug. The affection is a surprise at the start, but soon I relax and hug her back. Quick as she came, she leaves, her husband shaking my hand as he follows her out.

"Am I going to regret hiring her?" I ask Adam.

"Definitely."

We follow the sounds of laughter and friendly conversation out to the main office. As we reach the opening of the hallway, that cute little boy Mateo comes over to offer us empanadas from a plate that is almost too heavy for him to carry. Behind him, an older Hispanic woman reminds the boy to offer us napkins when Adam takes two of the piping hot treats, then she surprises me when she hugs me. The hug is great, a strong grandmotherly sort of thing that soothes my soul.

When she releases me, she gives my cheek a gentle pat and hugs Adam in the same way. They move on, Mateo offering empanadas to a group of hungry-looking volunteers.

"That's Rico's mom, Inez. She lives next door to Drew and Chloe." Adam takes a big bite of his empanada and hands the other to me. I'm in awe, too stunned to think about eating right now.

Like we've stepped up to a receiving line, others come over to greet us, each person taking a moment to hug me and Adam and pet the dogs. None of the hugs are quick and dirty one-armed jobs. We get proper hugs from Adam's sisters Ava and Anna and a hearty handshake from Anna's husband, Gary.

Mildred makes her way over too. The cane and neck brace force her into a rigid posture that slows her stride, but she refuses help as she comes to stand before me. I bend almost completely over at the hips to hug her gently as she says, "I'm just so terribly sorry about hitting you with my car. Doctors say I had a seizure, and I shouldn't drive again. I don't remember a thing, so I suppose they're right."

"I'm just glad we're both okay." I pat the old woman on the shoulders.

"If there's ever anything I can do to help you, you just let me know, okay, dear?" Mildred takes my hand in hers, giving it a gentle squeeze. The gesture is so sweet and motherly that it nearly brings tears to my eyes. I sniff them back and grin as a younger woman—who introduces herself as Mildred's niece—also hugs me, then leads her aunt away.

I turn to Adam and find his mom standing there, her arms wrapped around her baby boy's waist, apparently waiting her turn. When she comes to me and hugs me, I think I'm ready for the warmth and love I'll receive from her.

Nope. Not ready.

For someone so small, she wields the power to knock me off my feet, right off my axis. Her hug seems to shrink me down until I'm that sad little boy who just wanted the love and acceptance of his parents. And that little boy can't hold back his tears. I cry on her shoulder, letting myself feel my grief and relief, my pain and joy, and all the emotions in between. I don't know how long we stand like that, hugging as my tears wet the shoulder of her shirt. When we do come apart, she cups my cheeks in her hands, and I can see that our hug brought the tears out of her too.

We chuckle as we wipe our eyes. Adam wraps an arm around each of us and kisses our cheeks. His mom's gaze moves from me to Adam and back, and she smiles so wide. She pats her son on the cheek and tells him, "I told you so," before instructing us both, "I expect you two for dinner. It's chili tonight, so bring your appetites."

When she's gone and most of the other volunteers have wandered out through the newly hung door, it's just Adam and me in my clinic, standing arm in arm.

"What'd she tell you?"

"Huh?"

"She said, 'I told you so.' "

"Oh. She told me you were gay way back when she first met you."

I laugh and wipe the last of my tears away.

"You okay?" Adam asks, sounding a little more serious even as he smiles.

I look around at the space as the dogs explore every room and sniff every surface. Clearing my throat so I'm sure I can speak, I tell him the truth. "I'm great, truly…great. You?"

Adam smiles over at me and winks. "Never better."

EPILOGUE

ADAM

This is the second time I've been a groomsman at a wedding this year. Though, this time I'm a "bridesman," and I don't have to wear my starched firefighter dress uniform.

The dress code for today is white. Anything white. Everything white.

"It's a white wedding," Dee explains for the hundredth time to Drew and me, and we delight in pretending we don't understand the concept.

"I don't think that means what you think it means," I tell Dee as she butchers the chorus of Billy Idol's "White Wedding."

"Yeah, yeah. I'm no virgin. It's about new beginnings," Dee explains, and because Drew and I know this spiel by heart, we say the second part with her. "It's about fresh starts."

She scowls at us but grins a little when we laugh. Hey, we're just doing our part to keep the bride from getting nervous.

Outside, the weather has cooperated, too, dumping a thin layer of snow on the ground. It's a freak occurrence for central Texas to get snow in December, so the county fire department has had volunteer crews out all day, clearing and salting the roads to and from the venue so we can ensure Dee gets her dream wedding.

When the event organizer gives us the signal, Drew and I line up, alternating with Rico's brothers Javi and Manny to form the processional. Once the music starts, the four of us walk in with matching white linen pants, button-up shirts, and vests, each with a white rose boutonniere pinned to the lapel.

At the altar, we stand on either side of Watts, who sure has been busy officiating his fire station's weddings this year. Beside him, Rico looks stunningly handsome and a bit nervous in his white suit. Big back pats from his older brothers seem to calm his nerves as he smiles at us all and takes a deep breath.

I breathe deeply, too, as I turn and take a moment to look at the space in awe. Truly, it's lovely. The wedding is in the old Daughtry barn, which is probably close to one hundred years old. A massive space that used to be filled with horse stalls, it's all shined up to be a wedding and events venue now that the Daughtry grandkids sold the farm to a winery.

With festoon lights draped over the honey-colored oak beams above, the whole space is bathed in a warm golden glow. The new owners have lain wood floors over the stone dust, and chairs fan out from both sides of an aisle up the center, white rose petals dotting the bride's path.

Everyone, not just the wedding party, is wearing white. That old No-White-After-Labor-Day rule be damned, the bride threatened to kick out any guest who thought to rebel and wear red to her wedding. The visual effect of the honey-colored building and the warm lights with all that white silk and linen is gorgeous. Honestly, I didn't know Dee had it in her to create this living embodiment of a romantic Instagram aesthetic.

Part of me wants to film the event, but I promised Dee: no Rooster Crows appearances tonight. A couple months ago, I was arguing with her about that particular wedding rule. But today, I get it. I haven't posted much as Rooster lately, opting to keep my private moments private as I share them with my new favorite someone.

Speaking of that favorite someone… I scan the sea of white outfits and find him easily. I will *always* find him easily. He's my north pole, and my compass will always point his way. *Okay, that sounded really phallic.* I laugh at my own thought, and when my eyes alight upon Markus in that mass of wedding white, he's grinning, too, his celestial cerulean eyes bright with humor.

My hot vet sits in the second row, looking gorgeous with a trim white blazer over his shirt. At my insistence, Markus left the top few shirt buttons open, giving me a glimpse of his delectable chest. How could he deny me when I unfastened the buttons myself, on a quest to kiss that sexy little suprasternal notch between his clavicles?

Despite my efforts to tussle his dark hair, he's managed to tame it into a neat wave. The dark strands shine where they reflect the lights from above like a halo on the crown of his head. Damn, I've got it bad for this man, seeing heaven in his eyes and halos in his hair.

Markus is surrounded by my family, sisters on every side and Mom in the row ahead. Ava is closest, speaking behind her hand as she whispers into my boyfriend's ear. He chuckles at whatever she's said, so she repeats it for all my family to hear, laughing a little as they look at me.

What's so funny? I glance down to make sure my fly is zipped. It is, so why are they laughing?

My anxiety ratchets up with each word Ava whispers, but Markus shares a smile with me and winks. Just like that, the anxiety is gone. Markus has that power over me, the ability to keep me smiling like a dumbass in love. And that thought—that *L-word* thought—takes my mind in a new direction.

It's time. As of today, we've been official for six weeks, so I plan to take this opportunity to say something important: three important little words. But first...

Behind the audience, the big barn doors open to the snowy vista. The music changes—sadly, not to Billy Idol, but something classical—and everyone stands to turn and watch. Right on cue, Dee appears, flanked by her escorts.

My tough-as-nails LT looks ethereal in a gorgeous white off-the-shoulder satin gown. The tight bodice accentuates her lovely curves and extends down into a mermaid skirt, which swishes around her feet with each step she takes. Her long blond hair shines in this light and drapes in soft curls over one shoulder. The woman absolutely glows from the top of her golden head to the red soles of her white Louboutin pumps.

In one hand she holds a bouquet of white roses and orchids, and her father has his arm clasped with hers at the elbow. Mateo holds her other hand as he helps escort her to the aisle. After all, when you're marrying a single dad, it's not just the father you're committing to love and cherish—you're making a promise to his son too.

Mateo is proud of his role in the ceremony, and his smile beams brighter than the sun. He looks adorable in a white suit that matches his dad's. When they make it to the altar, Dee's father kisses her cheek and takes his seat, but Mateo stays with us, taking his father's hand so he's linked to both Dee and Rico.

Watts starts with stories about the bride and groom, how they met as kids and spent most of their lives in love with each other. Childhood sweethearts who separated for a time but finally found their way back to each other. There's even a funny story about the summer they volunteered to muck out the horse stalls in this very barn, only to do more making out than mucking out when no one was looking.

The stories are romantic and sweet and funny. When they exchange vows, Mateo pulls the rings out of his little pockets to hand to his dad and soon-to-be stepmom, and I tear up a bit. I've been tearing up a lot lately.

These past few weeks, it's like the blinders have been taken off my eyes, and for the first time I can see the love I share with kith and kin. From the mother and sisters I was born to, to the fire family I work with, to the community we all share: turns out, they care about me. They more than just *accept* me; most of the folks of Krause truly *love* me too.

That revelation brings tears to my eyes. And when Dee and Rico kiss, making this marriage official, a few tears fall down my cheeks. Lord have mercy! I'm crying at Dee's wedding. Pigs are probably flying around the sunset sky too.

After hugs and high fives around the altar, we groomsmen and bridesmen lead the way to the other end of the barn, where tables and chairs are set up for the reception. I find my seat, and my date, waiting for me at the wedding party table, and I give Markus a kiss as soon as I can.

"God, you look gorgeous in that vest," Markus says as he smiles against my lips. "It's giving me all sorts of naughty ideas about getting you alone in nothing but this."

He clasps his hands on the lapel of the vest to pull me in for another kiss, and damn, I really want to find a dark corner of this barn to start working on his plans. Though I can't help but add, "How would you feel about me coming to bed wearing just the vest and my Doctor Who socks?"

Markus throws back his head and laughs, then opens his mouth like he's going to say more. But before he speaks, Drew is on us, an arm around each of our shoulders so he can squeeze us together in a bear hug. "Ah, don't you just love weddings? And LT Dee looks so happy."

Drew has gotten so sappy since Chloe moved into his life. It's adorable. I wrap an arm around him and squeeze him back. "Speaking of looking happy… Where's your newlywedded bride?"

"Right here," Chloe says, and we pull away from our bro hug to make way for the little lady who is carrying a plate laden with brisket, a rack of ribs, and heaps of sides and fixings.

Leave it to Dee to serve barbeque at a white wedding.

My stomach growls, and I'm pretty sure I hear Markus's hunger rage too. Like he can read my mind, he clasps my hand in his, and we make our way to the food line. Once we have our own dinners dished up, we settle into our seats, tuck our napkins into our shirt collars, and dig into the food.

It's all very "couple-y," and I love it. I never in a million years would have imagined the bonded-pair life for myself, but I'm enjoying this immensely.

Interestingly, now that Markus is in my life, and he calls me Adam, a few other people have started to do the same. I hear people refer to us as "Adam and Markus" far more often than "Rooster and Markus." It's like I've graduated from my childhood nickname to my adult identity.

When we've finished our food and used the wet wipes placed beside each napkin to clean our hands, I reach for Markus. He laces his fingers with mine, filling me with warmth. Linked like this, we sit and enjoy the company as various people stand to give toasts. We all get a little tipsier with each clink and cheer to the bride and groom.

Once Dee and Rico cut the cake, I stand to go get Markus a slice of the sweet stuff, but the wedding band starts playing the song of the hour—Billy Idol's "White Wedding"—and Markus redirects me to the dance floor, explaining, "If I eat another bite, I'll explode. Let's dance some of the barbeque off."

Perfect plan. For my grand romantic gesture to work, the dance floor is exactly where I need Markus.

Weeks ago, I reached out to the band Dee hired to perform, and I requested a song. Now I just hope they added it to their playlist for the occasion.

Even if they haven't, we're still having a blast dancing with the other guests—mostly my sisters. We lose ourselves to the music, dancing to everything the band plays. Fast or slow, upbeat or down, it doesn't matter. We're having too much fun to stop.

The band slows it down a bit with Elvis's "Can't Help Falling in Love," and I pull Markus closer, wrapping him in my arms as we sway.

"This is perfect," Markus says as he glances around at the other couples dancing, then his eyes come back to me.

I look around too. The doors of this big barn are still open to the cold winter evening, but heat lamps set around the dance space keep us warm. Their blue and orange flames give movement to the shadows that dance in the old rafters and really bring this space to life. "It is. I didn't know Dee had it in her to plan something so romantic—"

"I'm in love with you," Markus says so fast it's like someone set fire to the seat of his pants.

"You. What?" *Wait. That was going to me my line.*

"I'm in love with you," Markus repeats with a little more air in his lungs and volume in his words this time. "You don't have to say it back. You can move on your own time. I just need you to know—"

"I'm in love with you too." I interrupt whatever other allowances he planned to give me. I don't need them. "I..." I laugh. "I planned to tell you tonight, but I was waiting for the right song."

"What could possibly be better than this song?" he asks as he sings along with Elvis and the wedding singer. As if the band is punking us, the keyboard player transitions from one song to the next, and it's the very familiar chords of the song I requested: George Michael's "One More Try."

"This one," I say and pull him just a little closer as he gives me the sweetest smile, and we move together along with the slow rhythm of his favorite song—now my favorite too. Markus leans close like he's going to kiss me. He's so near that all I can see are his eyes. All I can feel is his breath against my lips. I whisper, "I've fallen deeply, totally, completely in love with you, and every morning I wake with you in my arms, I fall some more. I'm proud to be yours and claim you as mine. I need you, and I want you, and I'm so goddamn lucky that I have you."

The air rushes out of him on a gust, and he sort of grins when he responds. "Wow. Same."

I laugh and it feels good. I feel good, lighter somehow, now that all those words are out. I kiss Markus, reveling in his familiar warmth and taste.

From somewhere behind me, I can hear my sisters hooting and hollering. Others join them as Markus and I stop any pretense of dancing and stand together—at the center of the dance floor in the center of this rustic old barn at the heart of our community in the heart of Texas—the world turning around us while we love each other.

The End

If you enjoyed the Hearts of Texas series, check out my Lost in Austin series for four emotional romances set in the bars and bedrooms of Austin.

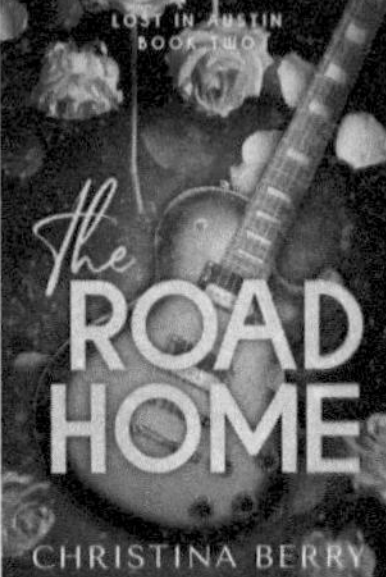

Love Triangle	Rockstar	Slow Burn	Grumpy Sunshine
Kink/BDSM	Roller Derby	One Bed	Friends to Lovers
Emotional Romance	Emotional Romance	Emotional Romance	Emotional Romance
Found Family	Found Family	Found Family	Found Family
Award Winning	Award Winning		

THANK YOU

Thank you for reading *Hearts We Claim*. If you enjoyed the story of Adam, Markus, Rufus, and Drusilla, please spread the word!

xoxo,
Christina

And don't forget to subscribe to my newsletter
or join my reader's group for
the latest news and new releases.

subscribepage.io/Td7TPB
facebook.com/groups/christinaswildberries

ACKNOWLEDGMENTS

When I started this book, nearly twenty years had passed since I had a dog in my life. I was going to have to do a lot of research to get the voice right for the Rufus and Drusilla characters. But then, the Universe's Cat Distribution System malfunctioned, and an adorable little Rottweiler/German Shepherd puppy came running up to my husband in the park across the street from our house. After about a week of looking for this sweet little baby's family, we concluded that *we* were her family. That was five months ago, and Zara has completely changed our lives for the better. Plus, Zara helped me get the voice right for my doggy characters, so thank you, sweet girl. And seriously, put your teeth away. No bites, just kisses!

Christina Consolino, my editor extraordinaire and author bestie, this book would not have happened without you. I cannot thank the Friend Distribution System enough for bringing us together.

Meghan Scott, Haley Cook, Tom Madison, and the guys at Fire Station #7—my helpful subject-matter experts—thank you for sharing your knowledge about medical procedures, veterinary practices, and firefighting.

Lizzie Stanley and Natalie Parker: y'all are the best author-buddies-turned-Zoom-buddies ever! Thanks for all the love and laughs.

To Meredith Tittle, who came into my life with an offer of PA help and who has been an absolute lifesaver in keeping me active on social media while I drown in book edits: thank you! I have so many ideas for promo moving forward, so get ready. ;)

Shauna and Becca at The Author Agency, thanks for your patience and understanding when I had to push this launch date a bit. It made all the difference.

A huge thank you to my friends and family for never balking when I'm deep in the writing trenches, and for provide heaps of hugs and laughs when I cave to the pressure and join you upstairs for karaoke night. I love y'all so fucking much!

Last but definitely not least, a thank you to my readers. You all are the absolute best. I love you, I love you, I love you! I have some pretty exciting ideas of what I'll be working on next, and I can't wait to share them with you!

ABOUT THE AUTHOR

Christina Berry is an award-winning author of smart, smutty romance. A citizen of the Cherokee Nation, Christina is originally from Tulsa, Oklahoma, and currently resides in Austin, Texas. When not writing, she can be found helping her husband with their never-ending home remodeling adventure or spoiling their amazing dog.

WWW.CHRISTINABERRY.COM

www.ingramcontent.com/pod-product-compliance
Lightning Source LLC
Chambersburg PA
CBHW030141010826
48973CB00002B/668